"I'M DISAPPOINTED IN YOU, FARGO."

"What?" He stared at her, brought back with a shock from the whirl of his thoughts to the fact that in front of him was one honey of a woman, entirely nude, and no longer untouchable.

She was looking at him strangely. "I remember you saying a nude woman brought out the beast in a man. I see no beast here."

His eyes squinted hard at her for almost a full minute, then he dropped his shorts.

"Do you see one now?" he asked. . . .

Bestselling SIGNET VISTA Books

THE TRAILSMAN 16

SAVAGE SHOWDOWN

by
Jon Sharpe

A SIGNET BOOK
NEW AMERICAN LIBRARY
TIMES MIRROR

NAL BOOKS ARE AVAILABLE AT QUANTITY DISCOUNTS WHEN USED TO PROMOTE PRODUCTS OR SERVICES. FOR INFORMATION PLEASE WRITE TO PREMIUM MARKETING DIVISION, THE NEW AMERICAN LIBRARY, INC., 1633 BROADWAY, NEW YORK, NEW YORK 10019.

SIGNET TRADEMARK REG. U.S. PAT. OFF. AND FOREIGN COUNTRIES REGISTERED TRADEMARK—MARCA REGISTRADA
HECHO EN CHICAGO, U.S.A.

SIGNET, SIGNET CLASSICS, MENTOR, PLUME, MERIDIAN AND NAL BOOKS are published by The New American Library, Inc., 1633 Broadway, New York, New York 10019

First Printing, April, 1983

1 2 3 4 5 6 7 8 9

PRINTED IN THE UNITED STATES OF AMERICA

The Trailsman

Beginnings . . . they bend the tree and they mark
the man. Skye Fargo was born when he was
eighteen. Terror was his midwife, vengeance his
first cry. Killing spawned Skye Fargo, ruthless,
cold-blooded murder. Out of the acrid smoke of
gunpowder still hanging in the air, he rose, cried
out a promise never forgotten.

The Trailsman, they began to call him all
across the West, searcher, scout, hunter, the man
who could see where others only looked, his
skills for hire but not his soul, the man who lived
each day to the fullest, yet trailed each
tomorrow. Skye Fargo, the Trailsman, the seeker
who could take the wildness of a land and the
wanting of a woman and make them his own.

*The untamed Dakotas,
land of the Sioux warriors,
early 1860s.*

Prologue

Just one more day, only twenty-four hours, and that handsome devil Skye Fargo would be back in town, Lily Baines thought dreamily, and she smiled with quick pleasure. Then she stretched like a cat in her big bed, aware that her body at eighteen, like a peach in June, had reached its peak of perfection. Yes, Fargo would be here, at the house, by the time she returned from her work at the bank. Her fingers stole down on her body for secret delight.

And she smiled again blissfully, for Skye Fargo had been her father's good friend, but her own secret love.

Today, she thought, will be a happy, happy day.

A cloud slipped over the bright June sun outside her bedroom window.

As she passed the mirror to reach for her undergarments, she paused, amazed at what magic nature had worked on her body just lately, giving her more curves than the road into Forked River. Her breasts were full, peaked with pink nipples, her stomach flat as an ironing board, and her hips curved out with womanly grace. Then there were her long shapely legs, her fine thighs, and between them the tuft of dark hair that modestly covered her virginal triangle.

She just couldn't help feeling a surge of pleasure, thinking how lucky she was to be given such bounty by nature. There wasn't a girl in Forked River who came anywhere near her kind of beauty.

She picked a blue cotton dress, her best, for it perked up the color of her skin, and it didn't hurt the shape of her body either. For Skye Fargo, nothing but the best. Fargo had ridden with her father, loved him like a brother, and when Dad was shot by that crazy drunk Tyler, it had sent Fargo into a towering rage. Good thing they had strung up Tyler in a hurry; God knows what Fargo would have done to him!

Lily sighed, thinking of her father; but that was two years ago, and Fargo had made it his business, from time to time, to drop by Forked River to be sure things were all right with her.

Ah, Fargo, Fargo. After her body began to push out, she secretly hoped Fargo would look at her with a different glint in his eyes. And, yes, on his last visit, he did say something, after staring at her breasts a long while.

"For God's sake, Lily, when are you going to stop growing those things?"

She smiled at the recollection as she went into the kitchen, where Aunt Tillie, her father's sister, had breakfast waiting. A dish of oatmeal, two eggs and ham, buttered biscuits and coffee. A full breakfast; she needed it, for she worked hard at the bank and also did her share of riding.

She finished breakfast, her heart singing, and started toward the bank.

On the way, she smiled at passing townspeople, gave a bright smile and a wave to Freddie Baker, who sat on his porch in a rocker, watching the flow of folks along Main Street. He waved back at Lily and thought about her for a moment. She'd become a real beauty, he thought, yet still was a sweet girl with a smile and kind word for everyone. Her dad, poor old Charley Baines, would have been very proud.

He watched her open the bank door, and then he got up and went into his house, and so he didn't see the three hard-looking men walk into the bank after Lily.

She turned, surprised. "The bank doesn't open till nine," she said. "You'll have to wait outside."

"The bank's open now," the biggest man said. "Just stand over to the side, missy, and look pretty, which is mighty easy for you."

She stared at him. He looked very dangerous; he wore a flat black hat and black shirt, and had big shoulders,

2

high cheeks with an ugly scar on one side, a slitted mouth, and dark shrewd eyes.

He also had a Colt in his left hand, and another gun in his right holster.

Her heart beat fast, but she was not Charley Baines's daughter for nothing.

"If you're planning to make trouble, I'd advise you, very strongly, to just get back on your horses and keep riding. This town knows how to take care of itself."

They all stared at her and laughed.

"How do you like this one, Clay?" asked the man with a big snout of a nose who was grinning ear to ear.

It was the big man who was called Clay, and his grin looked evil, with that slit of a mouth, as his eyes insolently went over her body.

"A beautiful bitch. Pity to waste it in this horse-ass town." Then he walked to the back, looked at the safe. He looked back at her.

"I don't suppose you have the key, missy?"

What she saw in his dark eyes made her afraid. He's a crazy man, she thought. I must not cross him.

"I don't have the key," she said.

Clay studied her, then nodded, his mind for the moment on the money.

"Pigface," he ordered the man with the snouted nose, "you take the door. Let them in, whoever comes. Then shut the door. Smoky, you stand near me and listen good."

She looked at Smoky, a lean, hatchet-faced man with a strange dead look in his eyes. He was staring at her, and she couldn't help but shiver. The sort of face that you might dream of in a nightmare.

The shades were still down on the windows. It was now two minutes to nine. She could hear the tick of the clock and also that of her heart. Parsons, the chief teller, and his assistant, Fuller, always appeared at the crack of nine, but they were not the sort of men who could face down men like these.

She thought of Fargo, and her heart lifted: if only he would come ahead of schedule. But it was still a day too early for him. She silently prayed.

3

She heard the sound of the door unlock and, as expected, Parsons came in with Fuller, followed by four men, all early customers ready to do bank business.

After the group entered, Pigface pushed the door shut.

Parsons stared at Clay, at Smoky, at the guns, and at Lily.

"What's all this?" he demanded, his voice shaky.

"I'm here to borrow a lot of money," Clay said, grinning and pointing his gun at Parsons. Frank Sanders, one of the customers in the back, reached for his gun, but Clay instantly shot him in the head. Sanders catapulted back, part of his brains spilling to the floor from where he lay. Lily wanted to scream, but in her fear she couldn't make a sound.

Clay kept right on grinning. "Nobody moves but us. I got an itchy finger."

He walked to the teller, Parsons, a well-fed, rosy-cheeked family man, staring at him with a sadistic grin. Then he asked politely, "What's the name, mister?"

The teller was grim. "Parsons."

Clay examined him coolly and then said, "Mr. Parsnips, I want you to meet my pal Smoky." The hatchet face came up with the dead look still in his eyes and stood directly in front of Parsons. When the teller timidly put out his hand, Smoky smashed his face instead with his pistol butt. Parsons went down, his nose spouting blood.

Clay motioned him up with his finger, and Smoky grabbed Parsons, pulling him back to his feet. Clay did not stop smiling.

"That's to keep you honest, Parsnips. Now get the money and put it into the sack." He turned to the broadsnouted man at the door. "Pigface."

Pigface brought over a potato sack, stuck it in Parsons's hand, and then went back to the door.

Smoky, holding the bleeding teller by the arm, pulled him back to where the safe was. Clay turned to Fuller. "You his helper?" Fuller nodded. "Then go help." Clay gave him a shove.

"Everything's nice now," Clay said, looking around with satisfaction. And he walked in front of one of the customers, a meek man named Jelks, and smiled genially at him. "I got no hard feelings," he said.

Jelks foolishly smiled back.

Clay stared at him. "What's funny, mister?"

Jelks looked confused. "I don't know."

Clay jerked a finger at the dead man. "A man just got his brains blowed out and you think it's funny." He raised his gun, pointed it at Jelks's forehead. "You don't have any feelings. I think you oughta join him."

Jelks began to tremble violently.

"Don't," he gasped. "I got a big family."

Clay stared into the man's eyes as if the fear of death in them gave him a kick.

"Oh," he said finally, "you got a big family. Well, I got feelings. I think I'll let you live."

He grinned, then, bored with Jelks, looked toward Parsons and Fuller, both stuffing money into the potato sack. "Hurry with the money," Clay said, then glanced toward the door and gestured to Pigface, who looked out and then nodded back an all's well.

Clay, as if to keep himself amused, now looked over at Willy Ames, a well-liked cattle wrangler who had been watching with a hard eye. Like the dead man, Sanders, he was wearing a gun.

Clay looked at him, and the slit of his mouth widened.

"What's up, little cowboy? I'll bet you're telling yourself if this coyote didn't have his gun out, you'd shoot him to kingdom come. That right, little cowboy?"

Ames nodded slowly. "That's right, coyote."

Clay's smile never changed. He put his gun in his holster.

They stared at each other.

Pigface and Smoky, both with their guns out, turned to watch, grinning. When Ames went for his gun, both men shot him; he went down like a slaughtered pig.

Clay shook his head. "You guys shouldn'ta done that," he said with mock gentility. "But I got no hard feelings."

Then Clay turned, his face now hard, "Mr. Parsnips, I'm not a patient man."

Parsons looked white as a sheet. "Almost finished. It's all we got."

5

Then Clay looked at Lily.

His grin came back, but it had also turned cruel. "I don't like the look on your face, missy."

She said nothing.

"Didn't hear you."

"I didn't say anything." Lily's voice was firm, her gaze steady.

His grin widened. "I'd like you to say something. Go ahead, I've got no hard feelings."

Still she stayed silent.

He stuck his head close, as if to hear her. "I'm waiting. I don't figure you think much of me."

Then, finally, she said, "I think you're crazy. And a killer and a coward."

His eyes slitted and his mouth went ugly. He didn't speak.

Then Pigface spoke from the door, warningly. "Clay!"

Smoky came forward with the bag of money, moved to the door alongside Pigface, and waited.

Clay ignored them, his eyes on Lily. "This filly has a lot of spirit." He moved closer to her. "Nothing I like better than to bust a bucking little filly." He turned to the others. "I'm taking her, Smoky."

"Sure, sure, Clay, but let's hightail outta here. People's heard the gunshots and are comin'."

Clay reached for her. She pushed him off. He laughed and grabbed at her. She clawed at the side of his face with her nails.

He put his hand to his face, looked at the blood in his palm. Then Pigface yelled from the door, "Clay, we gotta move!"

Then Clay hit her on the jaw and caught her as she went down. He carried her in his right arm as if she were weightless. He kept the gun of his left hand pointing.

When Mike Barry, the third of the customers who was armed, could stand it no longer, he went for his gun as the bandits were going through the door. Clay instinctively turned at the same moment and shot him in the heart. The man dropped heavily to the floor.

The few townspeople aroused and gathering at the door scattered as the three desperadoes came out with Lily, all

6

their guns blasting. They jumped their horses and rode hard down Main Street, their hooves thundering upon the baked red earth.

And Clay grinned evilly as he rode, still carrying the unconscious Lily as if she were only a sack of feathers.

After an hour of hard riding, they stopped in a pocket of boulders near a narrow stream. Clay looked at his horse. It seemed winded by the flight and carrying a double burden. Lily had regained consciousness and was carried before him in a tight armlock.

"Water the horses," he ordered to Pigface.

He dumped Lily down next to a boulder. She felt her heart thump as she watched Clay making preparations for the encampment. What he had in mind for her filled her with terror.

Smoky was showing him the sack of money; Clay looked into it without comment.

"It was a sweet job," Smoky said.

Pigface came up grinning. "Almost as sweet as this here sugar pussy." When he grinned, his snout broadened, making him look more than ever like a pig.

Smoky's dead eyes glanced at her, then he looked back at Clay.

"We can't stay here long," Smoky said.

"I know." Clay smiled, and he stared at her.

"It was a mistake to take her," Smoky said. "She slowed us down."

"Maybe she slowed us down some. But she's worth it," Clay said.

"Yeah," Pigface said, his eyes glittering, his mouth half open and drooling. "She's worth it."

"She's just a filly. And money is money. We don't have much time," Smoky said.

"She's not just a filly," Clay said.

"No sirree," said Pigface. "She's cherry. I'll bet my ass on it."

Clay turned coldly to examine him. "If she is, you won't be the first to know."

Pigface looked uneasy, but the stakes were high for

7

him. "She belongs to all of us," he said, hitching up his jeans. "You aim to keep her all for yourself, Clay?"

Clay studied him. "What do you think, Smoky? Is it a good idea to shoot Pigface?"

There was sudden ice in the air. Then Smoky said, "To hell with her. We've got the money. Let's hightail the hell outta here."

"No," Clay said coldly. "I didn't lug her here to leave her."

"I want a piece of her," Pigface said stubbornly.

Clay rubbed his chin. "I aim to dip in first. Then we'll see." He turned to her, rubbing his hand down over his already bulging crotch.

Lily shivered back against the smooth boulder. She had never had the experience of a man, and the last thing in the world she wanted was one of these cruel savages. Her heart beat like a frightened bird's. Could there still be some way to escape? She must surely try.

"Please, Mr. Clay. You've got the money. Why don't you go and leave me? I'll never breathe a word against you, I swear it."

Clay smiled, making the slit of his mouth look as though he were in agonized pain. He rubbed his cheek, still red with dried blood where she had clawed him. "I'm gonna have your scars, missy."

"I'm sorry. But you hurt me."

His voice became mocking soft. "Did I hurt you, dearie? I'm very, very sorry. But now I'm gonna hurt you better."

The other two men laughed.

He started to unbutton his jeans.

Pigface laughed again.

Smoky scowled. "Clay, we ain't got time for this. They'll have a posse. And besides, this is Sioux country."

Clay's eyes squinted at him. "I don't want to hear you again, Smoky, till I'm through." His voice was harsh.

Then Clay came toward her, staring at her breasts. "A beautiful filly with big beautiful tits," he said.

"Please don't," she said, rising, her voice pleading. "I've never been with a man."

He grinned wolfishly. "Well, you're gonna be your first time with a real big one, missy. You're lucky."

"Please, please." She turned and suddenly started to run toward the stream.

"Sonofabitch," Clay cursed, too dignified to run. "Get her, Pigface," he commanded.

Pigface took after her, tackled her near the stream, tore at her dress and her underclothing, quickly uncovering her breasts.

"My God!" Pigface exclaimed, his eyes glittering. He pulled at the rest of her clothes, and within a minute he had her stark naked and shivering uncontrollably.

He stared at her body, the sleek, silky skin, the full swelling breasts, the dark triangle, and he started to gibber to himself. Her body seemed to trigger something that made him go crazy. He tore open the buttons of his jeans, and she could see his obscene and ugly erection. He grabbed her shoulders, pressed her to the earth, pushed his knees between her legs, widening them, and thrust into her furiously, like an unleashed animal.

She fought, but he was an overpowering force. She felt him tearing inside her, sharp, intense pain as his flesh ripped into hers. Her hands thrashed about, felt the cold handle of his gun, and in an instant she had it out. She pumped the bullets, all of them, into his body, which made him jerk crazily against her in a final reflex. She looked into his eyes; they seemed to be squeezing right out of their sockets. And then he shuddered one more time against her and died.

It happened so quickly that Clay and Smoky seemed frozen in their tracks.

She pushed the limp body off, but her flesh was already covered with the blood gushing from his wounds. Her thighs were red with her own blood. The pain between her legs felt almost unbearable.

And then she sobbed.

Clay's face was stone as he came up to stare down at her.

Smoky swiftly brought up the horses. "Clay!" he said.

Clay pulled his gun.

She saw her death in his eyes.

"My friend Skye Fargo will cut out your heart, you bastard," she exclaimed.

"Fargo?" His face hardened. "But you'll never get a chance to tell him."

And he shot her in the heart, twice.

He climbed up on his horse, looked back at her, and said to Smoky, "I shoulda shot Pigface when I thought of it."

He spurred his horse, and they galloped away into the slowly darkening night.

1

Skye Fargo glared at the bruised ankle of his pinto and gritted his teeth, aware of the bottled rage in his gut. He stared at the trail as it twisted through the gorge, at the steep jagged rocks that hid the golden setting sun. He couldn't catch up with Clay, no, not yet. That killing bastard could live a while longer. His pinto, one of the great running horses, was hurt, and a man's life wouldn't be worth a plugged nickel if he was trapped in this territory with a lame horse. It meant that he'd have to put up precious days at Devil's Corner, a town he had bypassed earlier.

He sipped water from his almost empty canteen, but the taste of bitterness came more from his blocked fury about Clay than the water. He led his pinto toward the town.

Fargo's lean, hard-muscled body moved with the grace of a mountain cat. Under his broad-brimmed brown hat, the piercing lake-blue eyes in the sun-bronzed face restlessly, by habit, examined the trail. He shifted his Colt, worn in a low holster, near his strong, supple fingers.

By the time he reached Devil's Corner it had been dark for two hours. He stabled the lame horse at Brennan's, the smithy. He walked through the town's main street past Clark's Hotel, Grandma Mason's Café and Bread and Pies, and Grant's General Store, until he reached Flanagan's Saloon, Dance Hall, and Rooms, a ramshackle two-story house from which came the sound of a tin-eared piano.

The barman was stocky, wore an apron and a careful face.

"Whiskey, and leave the bottle," Fargo said. The first drink burned his throat, the second went down easier, the third eased the tiredness. He had been hard-riding more than a week and he could use the letdown, he realized.

He began to watch the card table, and it didn't take long to judge that a mustached, green-vested man the other players called Slade was a cardsharp; it was there in the way he dealt and fingered his cards. The money was stacked in front of him, and three liquored cowboys were his victims. Fargo didn't like it, but he wouldn't interfere. His job was to get Clay, and anything that slowed him down must be pushed aside. Also, Fargo felt it a man's own responsibility not to be fleeced, not to let himself be a victim. And it wasn't his job either, Fargo thought, as he sipped his whiskey, to right the wrongs of the world; there were far too many. He turned from the players. Besides, if he thought about it, most of his own muddles came from his instinct to help some poor slob in trouble.

It was then he saw the girl sitting with two other women near the piano. She couldn't be more than nineteen, yet unmistakably she was a dance-hall girl with that rose-colored dress and silk shawl. She had curly red hair, piled high, and white breasts that strained against her dress. He was wondering how such a girl, and so good-looking, had gotten into such fast company when she gave him a straight bold look, smiled, then got up.

"My name is Tess and I'm thirsty," she said.

She had green eyes that were steady and unafraid, astonishing in a girl that young, and the red dress clung tightly to a slender waist, a fine spread of hip, a flat tummy. Her young face didn't quite jibe with her developed figure, Fargo thought.

The barman put out another glass, and Fargo filled it. She tossed it off. She looked at him. "I said thirsty."

He poured another.

"I like liquor," she said, and her eyes went over him. "And I like strong men."

He felt the itch in his groin; he needed a woman, and this one looked like more than a taste of honey.

He smiled, and she smiled, too, her green eyes looking wise beyond her years.

"Looks like you've done some hard riding," she said.

He nodded grimly. "Yes, I've done some hard riding." And, he thought, I'd like to do more. He looked at her full lips, her full hips, and the bulging flesh of her breasts.

She smiled broadly, as if she had read his thought. "Yes, you look like a man who could use a letdown."

Damm, she was reading him; he had this fierce ache in his groin, and nothing would please him better than a letdown with this lassie.

"My name is Skye Fargo. Let's drink up."

She nodded slowly, looked hard into his eyes, then smiled. "You look mean, Fargo, but I liked the look of you when you came in."

His eyes moved slowly over her sexy body. "And I like the look of you, Tess."

She grinned. "Then what are we wasting time for? Bring the bottle."

Upstairs, she was a brazen little nymph, and when she slipped her dress off, he was pleased by the ripeness of her breasts, the whiteness of her flat belly and thighs, and the tuft of red between them.

He kissed her mouth, and she held him tightly. Then he went down to her silky smooth breasts, to a pink nipple, and put his tongue to it. She moaned a bit, and he knew she'd be a fiery little bitch. She twisted hard against him, and his hand went down to her mound, and she opened her thighs. She quivered as his fingers probed the soft warmth; he stroked her slowly, and her breath quickened. He stopped to pull off his jeans, and the sight of his huge erection made her sigh; her hand reached out swiftly and she gripped his maleness. She dropped to her knees, pressing her mouth against him, making small moans of pleasure. He watched, amazed at her skill, his body charged with tension.

"Fargo, Fargo," she whispered hoarsely.

He lifted her to the bed, where her white thighs spread, and he entered her slowly, feeling her body tremble as he worked himself deeper. Then her legs stiffened as he felt a surge of passion and thrust all of himself fiercely into her. "Oh, oh," she whispered.

She was tight, and he began to move around, holding her silken buttocks, and as he slid in and out, she squirmed about joyously. Each thrust made him aware that his thickness totally filled her. His rhythm of plunging quickened, and she whimpered like a little girl, as if the bliss was almost painful; but her grip on his shoulders was viselike, and he knew she would never let go until the end came. His increasing thrusts hurtled her to a great and shattering climax, and he felt the tightening within her, the smothered gasps of pleasure, and when, finally, he too had climaxed, her body shuddered like a leaf in the wind and she smothered her cries through clenched teeth.

For long minutes afterward, her fingers still held him with a strong grip, then slowly they unfastened. Her breathing came slower, and she lay at last silently beneath him.

Finally, she said, "Fargo, you're a mean lover."

He grinned. "You're not too bad." As he put his jeans on, he had to say: "How'd a kid like you get into this?"

She scowled at him. "Don't ask me that. I like it. I like liquor, I like loving. I don't apologize for it. It's how I want to live. Will that do, Fargo?"

"It's your life," he said.

He watched as she put her well-shaped legs through the silky bloomers, pulling them over her red bush and the white buttocks. She had one great body.

She read something in his eyes, for she smiled, patted her red hair.

"I hope we can do this again, Fargo. Before you leave town. It would be nice."

He nodded. "Yes, it would be nice." He tossed some money on the dresser.

She shook her head. "This one was for pleasure."

He smiled. "Take it. It's always nice to spend. Tell them downstairs I'll be keeping the room for tonight and tomorrow."

She left with a smile and a toss of her red hair.

After she left, he lay for a while, staring through the window up at the big stars in the night sky. Something about the girl reminded him of Lily, and with that came the fierce hatred he felt for Clay. Somehow, somewhere, he'd catch up with him and exterminate him, slowly, a piece at a time. The rage that streaked through his body made it hard for him to sleep, and he tossed fitfully in bed for hours before drifting off.

Next morning, after fried eggs and bacon, buttered hot

biscuits and steaming coffee at Grandma Mason's Café, he felt better and walked up to Brennan's, the smithy. The pinto tossed its head as Fargo picked up the foreleg. The ankle looked better; the swelling was down. Gently, he rubbed liniment over the bruise, then stroked the smooth, muscled flank.

"A great horse, Fargo," said the smith, a strong, barrel-chested man.

"A great heart," Fargo said.

"Should be ready tomorrow."

Fargo smiled grimly.

"Where you headed, Fargo?"

"Aberdeen and beyond." He looked hard at the smith. "I think a man called Clay came through here. Cheek scar, big shoulders, black hat and shirt, two guns."

The smith nodded. "Clay, yes, he wanted some saddle work. Came through about three days ago."

"Say where he was headed?"

"Didn't say. Friend of yours?"

Fargo's voice was even. "Just trying to catch up with him."

The smith's brown eyes glittered shrewdly. "Ornery, this Clay." He folded his muscular arms.

Fargo looked at him.

Brennan nodded slowly. "Some drifter bumped into him coming out of the saloon. Clay shot him dead. Just a drifter, a little bit drunk."

Fargo's lips tightened.

Brennan put a splinter of wood to his glowing forge and lit a cheroot. "Yes, an ornery gunman. Not a man I'd like to tangle with." He scratched his head, looked appraisingly at Fargo. "But I don't suppose it would stop a man like you."

Fargo shifted his weight uneasily. So, Clay had a three-day start—no, four. And was he really headed for Aberdeen?

"I'll need a horse for today," he said.

He rode the borrowed black out of town, picked up Clay's trail, made the necessary tracings on his destination, and decided it was Aberdeen. He stared at the long distances, he'd have to travel, the great towering rocks not far off he'd have to cross. The lonesomeness of the trail sometimes fashioned his mood. He was, he felt, a man who enjoyed the solitude of nature, and the sight of a hawk wheeling in the sky, the shape of a tree, the movement of a mountain lion, the glow of the sun when it hit the hills—these were things that often lifted his spirits.

The black was a good horse, but he missed the feel of his big muscled pinto beneath him. It was dusk when he drifted back to town, and it was beginning to look busy, with settlers picking up supplies for the long push west, a couple of Conestoga wagons standing near the hotel. The way some Easterners pushed into the territory, running the treacherous Sioux ambush, was openly suicidal, in his view. They didn't know, didn't understand, didn't dream the savagery in the heart of an avenging brave.

At the saloon, Slade, the green-vested gambler, had corralled three new victims, two young wranglers and a white-headed boozed-up old-timer. And because he had time to kill, because he disliked the man's mean eyes, the ugly slit of his mouth, and his dishonest ways, Fargo decided to sit in on the game.

Slade's small eyes scrutinized him. "Passing through?"

"That's right. The name is Fargo."

Slade introduced the other players, and they continued playing straight poker. The pots shifted around for a while, and Fargo thought that Slade had decided to play honest. Then Slade said, "Have a good time last night, Fargo?"

Fargo stared at him.

A leer came to Slade's face. "I mean the redheaded kid."

Fargo continued to look at him.

"Yup," Slade said as he shuffled the cards with his tricky style. "You should be grateful to me, Fargo."

"What do you mean?"

Slade grinned. "It was me that started her in this fun business. But I suppose it was easy. She had a natural talent." The men at the table laughed.

"Just deal the cards," Fargo said coldly.

Slade shrugged, and it wasn't long until Fargo found himself fed three queens. Once, when he had glanced away, he heard the whisper of a bottom card. The scuffle of a boot made Fargo glance up at the hard-faced, stubble-bearded man called Hawk by one of the players. Hawk watched the game with a man who could have been his brother. Then Fargo looked at Slade and read in the depths of his eyes a sadistic expectation. An ugly winner, and a man who didn't go with losing, he figured. He'd let his quarry win the pot, then set him up later. He knew he played better poker than Slade; most of the sharks, he had found, were not good players, depending on tricks for winning. He had done plenty of learning time with the riverboat gamblers and knew a couple of sharp tricks himself. So when Slade showed his flush, Fargo just lifted his liquor. It had been a big pot and almost cleaned out the others. The stubble-bearded Hawk, he noted, looked at the money with glittering eyes.

After several more pots, Fargo set up a couple of cards, picking up in the discards a couple of jacks; he did a fast cull shuffle, and after the cut he did a one-hand shift of the cut. He fed three tens to Slade and in the draw gave him another.

In the showdown there was almost a hundred in the pot, and when Slade put out his four tens, he grinned wolfishly and reached for the pot. His eyes went staring when he saw Fargo's four jacks. Then slowly he stood up, his face pasty and ugly. "What kind of a game are you playing?" he snarled.

"The same you are, Slade."

For a moment the small, mean eyes went blank, then they glittered with hate. Slade licked his lips. He didn't like the setup, but his hand was forced.

"What does that mean?" His voice was hoarse.

"It means you play a crooked game, Slade," Fargo said coldly.

The men at the table scraped their chairs as they pushed back quickly.

Slade's lip trembled, and small beads of perspiration on his forehead glistened in the light.

It was not a call that he liked, Fargo realized, because he didn't have the stack on his side. He was pushed and it was not a showdown he wanted, but he had to make his move; there were too many onlookers.

Fargo watched his eyes suddenly widen, his hand twitch, then dart down. His own gun exploded and Slade hurtled back as the bullet ripped through his chest, spurting blood.

There was an awesome silence as the men looked on death. Then the white-headed old-timer said. "That was the fastest draw I ever saw."

It's always the fastest draw when you survive, thought Fargo as he downed his drink.

2

He was passing the hotel on his way to Brennan's stable, thinking of his tracking of Clay, when he heard a woman's voice. "Mr. Fargo."

Standing in the doorway was a woman in long gray clothing, a white cowl covering her forehead. This so surprised him that he stopped in his tracks and stared. To see a nun like this so far west, and one who knew his name, was the last thing in the world he expected. His surprise seemed to amuse her, for she smiled. "Can we talk, up here, for just a few minutes?" She motioned to the porch, where a few battered chairs were lined up. Tied to the hitching post of the hotel were the horses of a Conestoga wagon.

Her knowing his name made him curious, and he came up on the porch as she requested.

"Please sit down, Mr. Fargo."

He put his bulk carefully into a rickety wooden chair while she sat in a rocking chair opposite. She was surprisingly attractive, he thought, with dark-blue eyes, a delicate face with a finely curved mouth, framed by her white cowl. The primness of her garment touched the expression of her face.

"I'm Sister Catherine. I know you're surprised that I knew your name. It was given me by Mr. Brennan, the blacksmith. I discussed my situation with him, and he thought that you might be helpful." She pointed to the Conestoga. "I am going down to Aberdeen with two sisters of our order. We had stopped in Twin Forks, where our guide, unfortunately, got drunk, picked a fight, and got himself shot. The country is wild out there, and we do need a guide. I understand you are headed toward Aberdeen. I'm prepared to pay you seventy-five dollars for

19

your help." She smiled engagingly, obviously thinking her offer would not be refused.

He stared at her. "You're thinking of going south in the Dakota Territory with two nuns like yourself?"

She frowned at the tone of his voice. "Yes, that's it."

He scratched his head. She was a pretty thing, but her brains must have been put in wrong. "That, good sister, is the dumbest thing I ever heard. You're talking of the meanest Sioux country, and the braves out there would make a feast of you. They would see you as women, not nuns. It's just the dumbest thing I ever heard."

She stared at him, and then her mouth went hard. "I was not asking for a comment on my mind. Just if you would be the guide."

He had to smile; she was a gutsy woman, but still foolish.

"No, I'm on business of my own. I'm sorry," he said.

"But you're going south toward Aberdeen. It wouldn't be out of your way."

"Yes, but he travels fastest who travels alone."

Her eyes went over his face, his body, his gun, and what she saw seemed to interest her. "The smith thinks you'd be very helpful to have along. Otherwise, I would not urge you. A hundred dollars is very good pay."

She had already and easily upped the ante; she seemed to have plenty of money on hand, and he wondered what the urgency could be all about.

"That's right, it is, Sister Catherine. But this country has no law—"

"We will trust in the Lord," she interrupted, smiling at him.

He smiled too. "Well, I trust in the Lord, but I keep my gun oiled."

She folded her hands primly. "I can see you're not a strongly religious man, Mr. Fargo. That's unfortunate. But it may be the hand of the Lord that brought us together to make this journey."

He stared at her. Sister Catherine was a beautiful woman under that gray drapery, and, in a way, it was too bad she had committed her life to purity.

"I don't think I made myself clear, good sister. Not only does this country have no law, but it has cutthroats and gunmen, and the Sioux, one of the meanest Indian tribes on the face of the earth. You'd be crazy to travel this territory without a cavalry escort."

Her eyes narrowed. "Mr. Fargo, you have an unfortunate way of expressing yourself. We are going, whether you do or don't. Nothing will stop us. The question is, will you or will you not be our guide?"

She was all guts and no brains. "The answer is no. I have my own business to take care of."

Her face was hard. "The smith told me you were a man, a real man. I think he exaggerated."

He stood. "You can think what you damned please. I tell you to wait for the cavalry."

"Don't worry about it, Mr. Fargo." She stood, too. "There are men who aren't all that fearful about gunmen and Indians."

She threw him a contemptuous look and went into the hotel.

Fargo's ears tingled as he loped to the stable. He was tired of this town of Devil's Corner, and nothing would please him more than to shake off its dust and this smooth-talking nun. Something about that woman got under his hide. Some women thought it was a man's job to do nothing but take care of their problems. Why in hell did she have to go galloping into the wild Dakota Territory like a chicken with its head cut off? That was a mystery to him. She could wait for a big wagon train of settlers to get protection; the more guns the safer the travel. It was even more a pity that because of her headstrong ways she might bring those other two nuns to grief. He had noticed in the Conestoga as he passed it two clear-skinned, attractive faces under garb similar to the other sisters, both looking out at him with undisguised curiosity.

"A real man," Sister Catherine had said. Women, even nuns, tried to hit you in the balls if you didn't go their way. He gritted his teeth; he decided he didn't particularly care for Sister Catherine.

At the stable, he examined the pinto with care. The swelling was down, and the animal seemed to walk all right, but it might be necessary to give him another rest day. Yes, it would have to be one more day.

The smith, Brennan, also thought it was best to wait. He was smoking a smelly cheroot. "I told that sister you were headed for Aberdeen. Hope I didn't speak out of turn, Fargo."

"No, it's all right. But I have some personal business that I want to wind up fast. A wagon like hers would slow me down too much."

Brennan nodded. "Just trying to be helpful."

As Fargo walked toward the general store in the twilight, he wished the smith hadn't been so helpful. The taunting face of Sister Catherine was now stuck in his head and he couldn't get rid of it.

He bought provisions from the general store, put them in his saddlebag, and then drifted back to the saloon. From the bar, he found himself watching one of the stubble-bearded men, the one named Hawk, at the card table. Hawk had a mean mouth that never smiled, and gimlet eyes; he seemed also to be having a run of bad luck, because the laughing apple-cheeked cowhand opposite him had coralled most of the money.

Fargo again looked at Hawk; the man made him think of Clay, and a bad feeling crept up inside him. He knew what that might mean, so he took a bottle up to his room, stripped to his shorts, and lay in bed. Before long the thought of Lily came floating back to him. Lily, that beautiful girl of old Charley Baines. He had ridden with Charley in his Forked River days, and he owed Charley, owed him plenty. And he knew Lily, too, had seen her suddenly grow up beautiful. A tender, brown-haired, sweet girl who never said a hard word to anyone, a loving girl, like one of those great summer flowers that gives its grace freely. And everyone cared about a girl like that.

And one rotten day she had gone into the bank where she worked in Forked River, and she was there when Clay and the two gunmen came in. They grabbed her with the money and fled. When the posse finally found her, she'd been raped, degraded, and murdered. And he stood at her grave as they piled the dirt upon her casket.

That bastard Clay! They had described him well: big

shoulders, black shirt, high scarred cheeks, a slit of a mouth, wearing two guns. Behind him, two men, one hatchet-faced, the other with a snout of a nose. They found the snouted one dead, near Lily, a pig of a man.

The ugly story, told to Fargo many times by witnesses, was burned into his mind.

He was already on a holy quest of vengeance, to hunt down the killers of his own family, but there was no way he could let a man like Clay walk the earth after what had happened to Lily.

Yes, Clay was indeed a fire that raged in Fargo's mind. It was a fire that would never be put out until he caught up with that killing bastard. He had finally picked up Clay's trail, and it was then his horse had gone lame. Fargo ground his teeth; the rage he felt now was the same that he had felt on the first day.

He lay there for some time, unable to digest the feeling, and took deep drinks from the bottle he had brought up with him from the bar.

Then he heard the soft step in the hall, and came alert. He had always been keen of eye and ear, and it was why he could survive alone in the territory; he could read the mark on a tree, the claw of a bear, the track of a deer, the print of the Sioux. You had to read signs as clear as a book if you hoped to stay alive. He knew instantly whose step was outside, so that when the tap came on his door, he said, "Come in."

It was Tess, and she wore that tight dress against which her white breasts strained.

"Thought you might want company," she said, smiling, shutting the door behind her.

He was sprawled out in his underdrawers, and her brown eyes went appreciatively over his body, stopped at his bunch-up, which even covered looked powerful, loaded with promise. He felt the liquor and the frustrated rage about Clay, a combination that put his body in a mood to explode. A woman like Tess could help put out part of the fire. She sat on the edge of the bed, smiling, and he grabbed her face, kissed her mouth hard and long, pulled open the front of her dress so that her full heavy breasts seemed to burst forth. He buried his face in sleek, silky flesh, then worked his tongue over the erect pink nipples, heard her moan softly. Then, almost brutally, he pushed her head down, and she eagerly jerked his drawers off his legs, thrust her face against his fierce maleness. Her hunger seemed to have no end, and she made small moans of ecstasy as she devoured him. Then, as she paused to throw off her dress to reveal her curving woman's body, he pulled her to the bed, feeling the full goad of his lust. He moved over her swiftly, and her thighs instantly opened to his prodding. As the blissful warmth enveloped him, he plunged inside her to the hilt. A groan of raw pleasure came from her lips. And now, lashed from within by a rage he could not express, he plunged again into her, and again and again, a relentless force that made her writhe and twist, as she felt the depths of her go tearing into frantic waves of pleasure. And when, after what seemed an intolerable time, he fiercely exploded, it sent a gush of joy vibrating from the center to every part of her body. She grabbed him against her, and only her clenched teeth could restrain the scream that surged from her throat.

She then lay quietly for a time beneath him, until finally she said, "Fargo, I don't think it will ever be that good again for me."

He just stayed still, feeling that for now, at least, some of the rage had been drained from his pent-up body.

It wasn't long after she was gone that he heard angry voices in the street, and before he reached the window, he heard the shot. Looking down, he saw Hawk, his gun out, and on the ground the apple-cheeked cowboy, part of his head shot away.

Fargo's mouth went hard. The cowboy was just a hardworking stiff who had made the mistake of winning from a buzzard of a man. He watched Hawk holster his gun and walk off with a swagger.

Just then the Conestoga wagon came rumbling down with Sister Catherine at the reins and two riders bringing up the rear. It was too dark now to see what they looked like, but they rode light and easy enough.

Fargo lay back on the bed, his hands behind his head. Well, it hadn't taken her long to find men who were not afraid of gunmen and Indians. She had more guts than brains, that was clear, but he had a bad feeling about what waited for her out in the territory.

He shut his eyes, and sleep hit him almost instantly.

3

Next morning, after a breakfast of johnnycakes and molasses, he saddled up the pinto and walked him nice and easy through the town's main street. At the saloon, he sensed eyes watching, but he kept his own gaze straight ahead.

The country stretched out in front of him, great grassy plains, edged with soaring hills and a sparkling blue sky specked with a few cottony clouds.

He felt a surge of pleasure, a man alone, with a strong horse under him, and with a whoop and a holler he gave the pinto its head.

It ran smooth as velvet, and it did his heart good to realize that it was good as new. He slowed the horse down to an easy pace, picked up the wagon tracks of Sister Catherine, and thought about her for a few uneasy minutes. After a time, he stopped, climbed a rock slope, and looked back at the horizon. He spotted a whirl of dust; two riders were behind him, he guessed. He rode on steadily till the sun hit hard in the afternoon, found a shaded area, and ate some beans and beef jerky. Then he climbed a rock and scanned the horizon again. There was again the faint whirl of dust. His mouth hardened. He calculated time and distance, then rode easy until the sun started down. He made camp at the edge of a grove of oaks with thick bushes. He ate slowly, watched the smoke of his fire swirl up, and smiled grimly. Sometimes, he thought, it was the right thing to let others know where you were hiding.

When the sun started to dip lower than the horizon and the light became gray, he got up and worked his way behind trees, skirting the trail that approached his campsite.

When he found a snug hollow in the ground behind a tree that gave good camouflage, he stopped to wait.

He waited patiently; long ago he had learned that patience was a key factor in survival. He could see a thin trail of smoke from his campsite, and every so often he heard the scurry of a small animal. He was watching a big red butterfly dart about crazily when the first crow went up. Then the second. He quietly slipped his Colt from its holster.

It took ten minutes before he heard the crunch of a foot on a twig. Then they came, two of them, stubble-bearded men, Hawk and his brother, guns in hand, stepping softly. They moved ten feet ahead of him, then stopped.

"See the smoke, Hawk?" the brother said in a low voice. "He's eating his beans."

Hawk nodded. "He'll be eating bullets in a few minutes. He won at least three hundred in the game. And he has plenty more. We'll be counting it soon."

"Start counting now," Fargo said, standing up.

At the sound Hawk wheeled to fire, but Fargo's bullet tore a gaping hole in his right eye, and he dropped slowly as if his spine had suddenly turned to jelly. The brother got off a shot that kicked the dirt near Fargo, then started to run, crouched low. Fargo's gun coughed again and the man seemed to dive into the earth, twist, and then lie still.

Fargo looked at them for just a moment, then started back to his campsite. Just a couple of prairie hyenas, he thought, who had decided Fargo had too much money for his own good.

Next morning he put his things into his saddlebag, mounted up, and followed the tracks of the Conestoga wagon.

Then he thought of Sister Catherine and remembered the last look on her face, one of scorn, and he gritted his teeth.

Why should it bother him? he wondered.

Still, he heard the growl in his throat.

The trail, he could see, twisted through a sea of yellow grass, sometimes coming near the shoulder of the mountain. Looking up, he could see crags, ridges, peaks of stone, and beyond it a cobalt-blue cloudless sky. The pinto moved along powerful and surefooted, but the sun burned hard and at noon he stopped near a stream, a campsite obviously used by Sister Catherine and her riders. The ashes indicated they were only hours ahead of him. In his study of the ground, he also found the track of an unshod pony, very recent.

He filled his canteens, watered the pinto, and gave him oats, which powered the horse much more than grass. Then he dived into the stream for a cool-down. Afterward, he dined on dried beef and sipped coffee.

It was then he heard the screech of a hawk and the squawk of a young bird, and looking up, he saw the hawk wheeling off from an attack.

Then he saw the young bird falling, its short wings spread in a futile effort to fly, which somehow softened its descent from the rocks high above to an outcropping ledge.

The hawk, Fargo realized, had dislodged a fledging, aiming at a quick appetizer.

As the hawk soared in circles, planning a swoop, Fargo waved his arms, which might have distracted it. Anyway, the hawk started to work its wings hard, as if it had suddenly spotted something tasty in the distance.

Fargo, squinting his eyes, now realized the fledging was actually an eaglet. It sat on the ledge thirty feet above him, and he could clearly see the proud beak, the crest of white, and stern black eyes, a bit ridiculous in a bird this young.

As he made the rocky ascent, climbing rock on rock, Fargo smiled. Was it humiliating to this eaglet to be nudged from its nest by a bird like a hawk? The eagle, majestic ruler of the skies, could still be very vulnerable when young.

The bird, after squawking twice, had squatted on the ledge that protruded from the west face of the mountain. The rock went steeply up with crags and furrows to a platform of stone, which joined to the east face of the mountain. A crevice there, Fargo suspected, would be the natural cover for an eagle's nest.

The eagle watched Fargo with its stern eyes while he climbed. Already, Fargo thought, the bird had the mark of magnificence about it, with that great beaked head. When he reached the ledge, the eaglet rose unevenly to its cruel-looking claws. Fargo cradled it in his hands, which soothed the bird, but he was thinking that hell would break loose if the mother eagle came back.

He made the ascent slowly, reaching the platform where the west and east face of the mountain come together. In a crevice of the stone, he saw the nest with the remains of two shells.

The damned hawk must have got the other babe, Fargo thought. As he stood there, eyeing the empty nest, suddenly the skin on his neck prickled—a primitive warning of danger. Was it the damned mother eagle about to tear his eyes out for molesting the sacred nest? No, it was something even more dangerous—a Sioux! Fargo saw him step out on the crag of the eastern wall, a bronzed figure, frozen, majestic against the sky. Broad of shoulder his body a ripple of muscle, and in his hand, held carefully, the twin of the eaglet that Fargo held in his own hand. The Sioux's face was strong, fearless, yet startled.

All this registered in an instant, for his hand flashed to his Colt, while the Sioux, with lightning speed, had his tomahawk back for the throw.

It was, for the moment, a frozen tableau, a white man and a red man with the instinct to destroy each other.

They stood with eye-to-eye contact, and something indefinable passed between them. Was it that both men had saved a young eagle? Was it recognition that in spite of being of different races, they recognized something alike in each other?

It was then that Fargo inched his hand away from his gun, and almost in the same instant, the Sioux slightly lowered his tomahawk. Fargo let his hand slide farther away, and the Sioux responded.

Then Fargo felt the rigidity go out of his muscles; he moved carefully, step by step, sideways, toward the nest, and put the eaglet in it. It squawked.

The Sioux's strong stern face softened, and he came forward easily on his moccasins and put the twin eaglet in the nest. The birds squawked together.

Then the Sioux turned and they were face to face. Fargo could see a scar on his cheek, sweat on the strong broad face. It was a face without fear, and in the black, burning eyes, Fargo felt, was the soul of a man.

Then the Sioux put his hand over his heart. When Fargo did the same, the Sioux's face again softened, and he turned and within moments was out of sight, down the east side of the mountain.

As Fargo climbed down the western side, he thought about this bizarre meeting. They had met as two enemies, yet they were brothers in spirit. And so, in spite of the war between their people, each had agreed to let the other live. And something even more had passed between them: what was it?

And then he heard the scream of the bald eagle, and looking up, he saw the mighty spread of wings, the great thrust of beak, the ferocious claws holding a half-eaten rabbit that it lowered into the nest for nourishment of its babes.

Still mindful that his pinto was just recovered from lameness, Fargo did not push too hard. And an hour before he expected dusk, he took his rifle from its saddle holster and picked off a well-fleshed rabbit. He skinned and fried it, and the smell brought a couple of buzzards floating overhead and a coyote who whimpered in the dark brush.

When night brought out its multitude of silver stars, Fargo lay in his bedroll, arms behind his head, staring at the sky. His stomach, fortified with fresh meat, felt gratefully full, and he dropped off. Not long after, he heard a soft movement near the campsite. His gun flashed and the coyote yelped and fell still. Part of the rabbit dropped from its teeth.

Midmorning of the next day, he picked up the whirling dust of Sister Catherine's wagon, and a bit after midday, the view from a crag made him aware of dramatic happenings at the wagon campsite. Two of the sisters were running, with a male rider in pursuit, swinging a lariat.

Fargo smiled grimly as he swung over the pinto. Sister Catherine's faith had to be a bit shaken if the men she had hired to protect her had instead decided to assault her.

The campsite, he had observed, was located within a

heavy thicket of bushes and trees. It gave them cover and would give him cover, too. He spurred the pinto, and it was a joy to feel the surge of power as it raced over ground.

He wondered what damage would be done by the time he reached the campsite. He felt searing anger at the kind of men who offered violence to women dedicated to a life of charity. His anger, however, never dulled his sense of survival. Before he reached the edge of the campsite, he dismounted, then crawled silently through the bushes until he heard voices. He crawled still farther until he could see too, and it was a sight to jar his teeth.

One man, a wrangler with blond hair, a red kerchief around his neck and grinning ear to ear, was holding Sister Catherine to the ground by her hands. And she, damn the devil, was stark naked, twisting her body this way and that. Her garment had been ripped from her and lay nearby. Facing her was a cowboy with short-cropped black hair and a black mustache that did not hide the white of his grinning teeth. Off to the side the two other nuns, young things, with wide, frightened eyes, were tied to a tree.

The man with the mustache was making what he obviously considered a very civilized offer.

"Now Sister Catherine. We don't mean to do this, but you're forcing our hand. Just tell us where you hid the money and we'll let you go. All of you."

She stopped twisting. "It's God's money, not mine to give. Please, please, Mr. Gibson, let me get up."

"But God's money belongs to all of us," said Gibson with reasonable logic. And looking at her body, he licked his lips.

Fargo, from where he was, almost licked his lips too. She had, as he would never have guessed, one of the sexiest bodies a man could hope for. Shapely, well-rounded breasts, a flat tummy, blond hair in the triangle, lovely slim thighs and legs. The hair of her head, almost golden in the glinting sun, cascaded down over her fine shoulders. She was a feast for any man, and the pity of it, Fargo couldn't help thinking, was that men were prohibited from enjoying it. But Gibson, of course, seemed to have his heart set on enjoying it anyway. There was no doubt in Fargo's mind that once Gibson laid his hands on the money, he would lay his hands on the rest of her. And after finishing with her, the two lovely young sisters who quavered in terror, tied to the tree, would be ravished as well.

Although Fargo felt pity for the trembling young women, he did not think the moment right to interrupt the festivities.

The man holding Sister Catherine would be no problem, for his hands were engaged. As for Gibson, he'd be less of a threat once he started his sexual assault. That sort of thing, as Fargo well knew, made a man concentrate hard, and made him extremely vulnerable.

So Fargo watched with very lively interest.

"I can't give you God's money, Gibson. I beg, for your sake, that you stop this. God will take a terrible vengeance."

"Do you think so?" Gibson asked. "But maybe a woman like you would be worth it."

"No, no, please. Don't do this, Gibson!"

"Hold her, Rusty."

"I'm holding," said Rusty, grinning evilly. "Just leave some of the meat for me. Ever seen anything this good?"

"Leave something for you?" Gibson laughed and jerked his fingers at the other girls. "You'll wear your tool out. Just hold this one." And he pulled his jeans down, his throbbing erection obscenely jumping out.

Sister Catherine screeched. "Wait, wait! You can have the money."

"Where is it?" Gibson demanded, holding on to his jeans.

"Sewn in the hem of my dress," she said.

Gibson stared at her. "That's very sneaky of you, Sister Catherine. It's no wonder I couldn't find it." He looked at her, drooling a bit. "I forgive you, sister." He stroked his chin, then looked down at his arousal. "But I do have hard feelings about you. And I'm just about to let you have them. Hold her, Rusty."

And Gibson got down on Sister Catherine's body, trying to push her thighs apart, to pierce the lush blondness. She screamed, twisting this way and that.

"Oh, shut up," Gibson said and slapped her face hard.

32

"That's not very nice, Gibson," Fargo said, quickly stepping out into the clearing.

There was a paralyzed moment when everything went still. Fargo's eyes were on Rusty's hands, which snaked to his gun. The Colt barked and Rusty, with a hole in his forehead, dropped like a sack of potatoes.

A cry came from Sister Catherine as she pushed Gibson from on top of her. His pants were down at his ankles, and he fell. Then he turned and raised his hands. "You caught me with my pants down," he said, smiling.

"Pull them up," said Fargo, holstering his gun.

Gibson's eyes glittered. "It was just a little fun, trying to scare a bit of money out of the sisters. That's all."

"Oh, was that all?" Fargo said agreeably. "Well, perhaps she has a sense of humor. So, why not apologize and be on your way."

Gibson grinned. "You're a good scout." He turned to Sister Catherine, who had grabbed her clothing and was trying to cover her nakedness. "I apologize, sister. I'm afraid I got carried away—by greed." He turned to Fargo, smiling as he pulled up his jeans, hitching them this way and that, and when his hand got close to his gun, he went for it.

Fargo's first bullet hit him in the groin, and the second struck his heart. He fell back as if he'd been poleaxed.

Sister Catherine stared at Gibson, her persecutor just a few minutes ago. She was holding her habit over her body, but somehow the left breast still showed. It was very distracting to Fargo.

Then she looked at Fargo. "I told him, I told him, that God would take a terrible vengeance."

Then, aware that her breast was bare, she covered it quickly. Her blue eyes met his for a long moment. "Thank you, Mr. Fargo," she said simply.

He untied the other two sisters and was jarred by how tightly they hugged him, especially Sister Teresa, who made him embarrassingly aware of the size of her breasts. There should be less flesh on women devoted to the world of the spirit, he thought. He felt masculine urges and figured it would be a hardship traveling to Aberdeen with women like these.

But he couldn't very well let them make the trip alone.

Sister Catherine's judgment about the right escort had pushed him into the role of protector.

"You were a godsend," said Sister Teresa, who was pretty, red-haired, modest, with that surprising heft to her breasts which her gray cloth could not conceal.

"Oh yes, thank heaven you came when you did," said the other, Sister Elizabeth, black-haired, dark-eyed, with delicate features that kept smiling.

"I'm sorry," said Sister Catherine, now clothed and wrapped in her usual dignity. "I thought Gibson a man you could trust. He acted so respectful—he looked so protective."

Fargo felt a spasm of irritation, mostly with her. Now he'd have to travel with a slow wagon, which would delay his showdown with Clay. And just to ride shotgun with a wagon through this territory meant trouble.

Some of his irritation crept into his voice. "I told you this was wild country," he said to Sister Catherine. "You can't put your trust in any two-bit sidewinder whose face you like. I told you to wait until you had a cavalry escort."

Sister Catherine stared with frosty blue eyes. "Mr. Fargo, I'm very grateful for what you just did. And I made a mistake about a man. But it's not all that shameful to put trust in a fellow human being. And I know it's a wild country. That's why the sisters and I have come here. Perhaps we can help civilize it a bit."

Fargo gritted his teeth. Blast her hide. She was dead right, but she talked like a schoolmarm, and if she weren't wearing that cloth, he'd lift her skirt and spank her bottom red.

Instead, he kicked a stone, grumbled, then took the guns from the dead men and threw them into the wagon. He hoped the women could shoot, but for the moment he said nothing about it. They just had had their pants scared off, and there'd be no point telling them they were riding into a terrain where anything could happen.

Sister Elizabeth had been watching him. "I'm sure Mr. Fargo wasn't being mean, Sister Catherine. We may be interfering with his plans. You did tell us he was in a hurry to get to Aberdeen." And she smiled.

Fargo couldn't help smiling back at her. She seemed to

be the kind of woman who could laugh despite the fact that only a few minutes ago, she was facing, with the others, rough-and-ready rape. And she, at least, showed some understanding of his situation. But that stiff-necked Catherine was a prune clear through, even if she had right on her side. Deliver me, he thought, from a righteous woman.

"Well," said Sister Catherine, "if Mr. Fargo is in that much of a hurry, he can just go on. We'll take care of ourselves."

She motioned the sisters to climb onto the wagon. Then she said, with a meaningful smile, "But I can't believe any red-blooded man would leave three women alone out in this savage territory."

Fargo shook his head. She was a ballbuster of a woman, this one. "I just hope," he said, "that my blood, whatever its color, is still in my body at the end of this trip."

He hitched up his jeans. "Now, Sister Catherine, will you get behind those horses and get your wagon going."

Then he whistled for the pinto, and the horse came trotting up and nuzzled him.

The more he saw of some women, the more he liked horses, he thought, as he swung over the pinto.

4

Fargo rode ahead, his eyes restlessly scanning the terrain. A lone wagon, he felt, was less conspicuous than a wagon train, which could hardly escape the eagle eye of the Sioux, and always unleashed their fury.

They traveled the flatlands, through great growths of wheat grass, over hillocks, and when the clouds gathered, they picked up, to the south, a slight drift of smoke.

Fargo led the wagon to a tree cluster where the horses could feed and water, then went on. He tethered the pinto where it could forage, then crept through waist-high grass until he sighted four men, heavy-bearded, heavy-fleshed buffalo skinners, sitting around a small fire. They had just finished a dinner of smoked meat; they wore big hats and checked shirts and were drinking from a whiskey bottle, which they passed from one to another. They talked in monosyllables, drank, and stared into the fire.

When he returned to the wagon, Sister Elizabeth, with anxious eye, asked, "Was it the Sioux, Mr. Fargo?"

"Buffalo hunters," he said.

"Oh," she sighed, relieved. "At least they're not savages."

Fargo grimaced as he pulled the saddle from the pinto. Not savages, he thought, but more dangerous. Men like these killed buffalo mercilessly, for the skins only. A Sioux killed only what he needed, using the meat of the buffalo for food, the hide for clothes, the horns, even the organs. Who was more savage, he wondered, the man who killed for need or for greed? And when it came to women, woe betide the one who fell into the clutches of a buffalo hunter. But there was no point, Fargo decided, in throwing a scare into the sisters. Nothing could be more deadly than traveling with frightened women. He had to admit, however, that Sister Catherine had showed a lot of nerve when Gibson tried to put the screws to her.

His mind flashed back to her shapely breasts and that lush blondness, and he shook his head to erase the image. It was a hell of a time to get horny when the only women available were strictly not available.

He sighed and put the saucepan with its beef stew over the fire. Sister Catherine had spiced the stew with herbs she found nearby, and the meat tasted delicious.

The moon, round and golden, hung low in the dark sky, throwing warm magic light on the tree clusters and the jagged rocks that stretched for miles along the trail.

Because the night was too warm for sleeping in the wagon, the sisters brought their blankets out and slept under the wagon. Fargo, to give space for their modesty, took his bedroll to a patch of bushes out of sight.

Next day Fargo rode in front of the wagon looking for signs that would betray the presence of man. He stared hard at rock formations and crevices that offered concealment, and at the trail.

They traveled at a steady pace until the sun hit the rim of the canyon, at which time Fargo rode back to join them. A glance at the right horse indicated it was favoring its left foreleg. He held up his hand, and Sister Catherine brought the wagon to a stop. He threw her a hard look. "Can't you see that horse is lame?"

Her eyes widened. "No, I didn't notice."

"What do you notice?" he asked.

She glared. "I notice rudeness and bad manners."

"It would be better if you noticed the horses instead," he growled. When he pressed the leg, the horse whinnied.

"This leg will need four days of rest," he said.

She stared, dismay on her face. "Four days! We can't stay here four days."

He thought for a moment. There was a corral, if he remembered rightly, at a place not far from here called Twin Oak. "I'll have to get a horse. At Twin Oak."

Her eyes glowered. "Are you thinking of leaving us in this wild?"

"No, we can't do that. You might be attacked by a

gang of rabbits." He brought the wagon to an opening sheltered by overhanging stone. "I'll be back in about three hours. Don't wander in the area, don't start a fire. You'll be all right."

Although he had jeered at the anxiety Sister Catherine showed at the idea of being left unprotected in a corner of a wild territory, Fargo felt he should dispatch his business in double-quick time. He pushed the pinto hard, and the heat of the sun brought froth to the horse's mouth. He stopped briefly at a river crossing to cool down the pinto and wash the sticky sweat from its body.

It was late afternoon when he reached the wooden bridge just on the outskirts of Twin Oak. As the hooves of the horse drummed over the wooden planks, Fargo could see, not far off, six horses feeding in a corral. They belonged, he had heard, to the proprietor of the Last Chance Saloon, a man called Phelps, who traded and sold horses. He liked the look of a strong-chested sorrel feeding in the far corner. He cantered to the saloon, swung off the pinto, and reined it to the hitching post, where two other grimy, sweaty horses stood.

He walked through the swinging wooden doors of the saloon to the end of the bar. He often took this position; it was an instinct for survival. An outpost such as Twin Oak, he thought, would attract low-down drifters and desperate men. There were two men at the bar drinking who, to his mind, fit that description. One was a big man with a red stubbled beard and hard eyes under a beat-up Stetson. He was booted and spurred and wore a Remington. The other had dark eyes and a narrow face and wore a Colt, strapped high.

Fargo smiled pleasantly, but they coldly nodded, then turned to each other.

"Whiskey," he said to the barman, a bald-headed, florid-faced man, who came up with a rag to mop the counter. Fargo dropped a double eagle on the counter.

"Anything smaller?" asked the barman, staring at it. The two men turned, scrutinizing him with more interest.

"There's a sorrel out there I like," Fargo said, "and I'd be pleased to offer these men a couple of drinks."

The barman, Phelps, grinned. "Nothing wrong with that deal, mister."

"The name is Fargo."

The redheaded man brought up a smile, showing a couple of black teeth. "Mighty nice of you, Fargo. Don't you think so, Chuck?"

"Yes, I think so, Red. Mr. Fargo appears to have horse trouble. That right?" Chuck said.

Fargo looked into the dark mocking eyes and saw mischief an inch deep.

"Right smart for you to know that." He drank his whiskey. It went down smooth; Phelps had pulled booze, not rotgut.

"Got a bustdown, is that it?" Red persisted.

Fargo felt a tinge of regret that he had played his hand so fast. The double eagle had unleashed greed in these hyenas, and they suspected there was more where that came from. But his hand was forced because time was short; the wagon and the women were sitting ducks for trouble, and the quicker he got the horse back, the better. There was no question that the sudden interest of these two trail scavengers would set up a roadblock.

Phelps stepped in, trying to ease the tension. "I hear there's a Sioux hunting party east of here."

"How'd you hear that?" asked Fargo.

Phelps mopped his counter. "Two cavalry men stopped in on their way to join their company. There's a load of wagons they say, coming west, and it could run into Sioux trouble."

Red hit the counter with his glass. "Damned redskins, we ought to burn out every last one." He stared at Fargo, who was looking at the poster of a buxom blonde in pink tights behind the bar. "Hey, Fargo, don't you think so?"

"Don't I think what?"

Red gritted his teeth. "I say we ought to wipe out all that redskinned trash."

Fargo looked at the heavy-lidded brown eyes with the dirty whites, which seemed to have no depths, no feeling.

"We're pushing them off their land," he drawled. "A man wouldn't be much of a man if he didn't fight for his land."

Chuck put his hat on the counter. "I didn't figure you for an Injun lover."

Fargo looked at the two men with their mean faces, their leering mouths. "Well," he drawled, "I ain't no lover of white trash, either."

The men stiffened, and Phelps spoke quickly. "This round is on the house, men." He poured whiskey into the glasses.

After an uneasy moment, Chuck picked up his drink.

Phelps poured a glass for himself and looked at Fargo. "I gotta say you know how to pick horseflesh. That sorrel has a lot of stamina."

"I can use it," said Fargo.

Red's eyes gleamed. "Got a wagon bustdown, is that it?"

Fargo lifted his drink. "I like traveling with a spare horse, in case there's trouble with one."

Red slapped his thigh and roared. "Well, there's a mighty careful fella. Don't you think he's careful, Chuck?"

Chuck grinned. "Yeah, and it's a good thing to be careful. I mean, you live a lot longer."

"Yeah," said Red, turning to face Fargo straight on. "Now, my good friend, if you just put the rest of your double eagles on the counter, you can go on living." His voice was soft. "But be very careful. I mean, your gun." By this time, Chuck too had turned to face him.

Fargo stared at them, a smile on his lips. But the bartender was reading something else in his eyes, because he flattened himself against the wall.

"Well, to be real honest, I just don't have enough of these double eagles to share with you. So why not be good fellas and forget it. Let's drink up."

Red's face went hard. "Hey, Fargo, you're being real stupid. We've got you, two to one. There's no way you're going to come out whole. Just put the double eagles on the bar. And don't make a wrong move."

What Red and Chuck saw suddenly in his face made them go for their guns. Fargo's gun coughed twice, though it almost sounded like once. Red never cleared leather, but fell with his chest ripped open and bloody.

Chuck had just cleared, but he dropped too, with a fast bullet in his heart.

Fargo looked at them lying on the floor in a rapidly widening pool of blood. He picked up his glass.

"Love of money is the root of all evil, Phelps."

Phelps, a bit white-faced, nodded slowly. "That was very fancy shooting, Mr. Fargo."

Fargo hitched his belt. "I'm sorry to mess up your floor, but I have to get moving."

"That's all right. I'll give them the kind of burial they deserve." He poured a drink. "Have one on the house. Just between us, Fargo, they were aiming to pick my bones before you came in. Much obliged. Take the sorrel, whenever you're ready."

The sun was down to the horizon, a great red ball touching the sky with flame, by the time he reached the wagon. The sisters were delighted at sight of him, he could tell, but Sister Catherine, if she felt anything, scarcely showed it.

She watched silently while he unhitched the lame horse.

"What happens to it?" she asked.

"He'll be all right. He'll go wild, find some friends."

She scowled. "Unless the coyotes get him."

"They might," Fargo conceded. "That's the law of nature. But he might be lucky."

Her lips were pressed. "The law of nature can be very cruel. Can't we take him along? He won't have to pull."

"He's lame. If he has to run, it will destroy him. The legs are the weapon for a horse. He'll be all right. Now, let's have some supper. We'll get up early to make up for lost time."

He dug a hole so their fire would not be seen, and they ate jerky, baked potatoes, and beans.

After dinner, he watched the three women as they sat around the fire. The sky was studded with big silver stars, and the shadow of the mountain bulked up like a hump-backed monster.

Sister Teresa, the redhead with the impressive chest, was smiling.

"We're lucky you joined our party, Mr. Fargo," she said. "It's hard to image what would have happened with-

41

out you." Her smile, he thought, had very little spiritual quality; she seemed worldly, like someone with lust of the flesh. And with her deep breasts, she was clearly miscast as a sister. He sighed. The sight of Sister Catherine, nude and defenseless, on the verge of violation, was not something he could easily wipe out of his mind.

"Oh, yes," said Sister Elizabeth with her ready smile. "It's twice now that you stepped between us and a very dangerous time. We're very lucky."

Sister Catherine did not appear too happy at what she felt were the excesses of her charges. "I think we can thank Mr. Fargo for his efforts. But isn't it clear that what you call luck is more like the hidden hand of our Lord?" She looked at him with her bright blue eyes. "Heaven moves in mysterious ways. Perhaps Mr. Fargo has been chosen to help us reach our destination."

He grinned. "I am, then, in your opinion, a tool of heaven, to bring you where you have to go."

The sisters tittered, but Sister Catherine just glowered. "You may find it amusing, Mr. Fargo, but even the scoffer may be used for divine intention." She turned her tin cup to let the coffee grains drop to earth. "And we must believe it is not God's intention to let three women be lost in the wilderness."

Fargo shook his head. She had a hell of a faith, and he was not one to jeer. But the world did have a hell of a lot of wickedness. Men like Clay, who had destroyed Lily in one crazy moment, Lily, who was the soul of goodness. What had been the intention of heaven then? It was a mystery. Well, he had seen death quick and sudden most of his life, and good men died as easily as bad. The thing was to keep your gun clean and your wits sharp.

He stood up. "It's a good time to get some sleep in this wilderness now."

5

Riding on the afternoon of the next day under a fierce sun, he suddenly reared back on the reins of the pinto, his nostrils assaulted by the stench.

"What is it?" Sister Catherine asked, with distaste.

"Buffalo," he said grimly.

Later they came on the buffalo, at least fifty carcasses, slaughtered and skinned. The bodies, big, black hulks, lay in the sun while sharp-beaked buzzards tore at the flesh. Fargo stopped to stare at a massive head, grotesque against the earth, its skull partly shattered by the force of the big buffalo gun.

It was a desolate spectacle, and he felt a swift rush of rage. He'd seen them, earlier, the buffalo killers in their camp, hard-faced and gross men with heavy rifles. They killed only for the skins. The meat, now wasted, could have fed an Indian tribe or, for that matter, a wagon train of settlers for months.

"How pitiful," said Sister Catherine, her eyes shining with pain. "Who did it—Indians?"

"Buffalo killers, hyenas walking on two feet," he said. He had scouted the ground, picked up the heavy prints of the buffalo men and their horses. Four, headed southwest. Then, to his surprise, he picked up freshly made prints of a moccasin and an unshod pony. An Indian tracking the buffalo men, southwest, across his own damned trail. That could be a hell of a tangle. He'd have to scout it. He brought the wagon to a camping site near a stream.

"I won't be gone long," he said.

"What?" Sister Catherine frowned.

He squinted at her.

She glared. "Where are you off to now?"

He dug his finger into his ear. "I'm going to scout a bit."

"Scout a bit? And while you are trotting around, we sit here and wait and wait. We are trying to get to Aberdeen, Mr. Fargo."

He scowled. "Let's get one thing clear, Sister Catherine. There's one boss here, and that's me. Do you understand that?"

Her light-blue eyes threw off sparks. "I understand it doesn't take much to turn you into a bully."

He gritted his teeth. "Listen. You hired me to get you to Aberdeen. I'm trying to do that and keep you in one piece. To do that, I must make sure we are moving into safe territory. Is that clear now?"

There was a twist to her pretty mouth. "I don't think, Mr. Fargo, that I'll be clear until we reach Aberdeen."

Why, he wondered, did this woman make him grind his teeth so much? "In case you need them, you have the guns. But I'll be back soon."

He took up the trail, following it over convoluted terrain for almost a half hour until he heard sounds softened by distance. He tethered the pinto to a low branch and, crouching low, went through the grass. When he heard harsh laughter, he began to crawl until he reached cover.

Soon he lifted his head. Four buffalo men, one with a knife, surrounded an Indian brave tied to a tree. The same Sioux, broad-chested, in a breech clout, the one he'd seen earlier with the eaglet on the crag. Somehow, the buffalo men had picked him off, and now they were interested in a bit of blood sport.

Fargo's jaw clamped hard as he watched.

The Sioux's face was proud and his lips were twisted with scorn. A four-inch cut on his chest slowly leaked blood. The man with the knife, ferret-faced and grinning, turned to the big muscular man in a red-checked shirt. "Why don't I hit his balls now, Lonnie?" he said.

"Too quick, Jim," Lonnie said, studying the Sioux. "I want to wipe that look off his face slow, a little at a time. And work down, so that he knows what's coming."

"That Injun is gonna go without a sound," growled a bearded man in a big Stetson.

Lonnie looked at him. "I've got fifty dollars, Sam, that we break him down."

The bearded man examined the Sioux, whose face was like granite. "All right. You got a bet." Lonnie leaned forward, his eyes glittering with excitement. He nodded to Jim, who grinned fiendishly. "Let's play tic-tac-toe," Jim said, and he cut slowly with the point of his blade across the chest, making four thin lines of blood.

The eyes of the Sioux narrowed, but he did not flinch.

"Might as well be writing on leather," said the bearded man, grinning.

Lonnie's cruel eyes studied the Sioux. "We'll see. Put my circle in the middle box, Jim. If you win, he's all yours. But not too quick—I've got fifty bucks riding here."

The Sioux, thought Fargo, watching, had already given up his life. He looked calm, fearless.

"Cut deeper," said Lonnie.

He'll never break, thought Fargo, pulling his Colt. He was going to help the Sioux, even though it meant war on his own kind. But there was no kinship with men like these. He felt more of brotherhood with the Sioux, who was enduring and brave, than with this human junk who exploited the territory and murdered for fun.

"I told you, Lonnie," said the bearded man, "this one won't break."

Then a fourth man, thick-necked, big-bellied, strode up with his knife. "I'm gonna make this redskinned bastard sing like a canary. I'm gonna cut his balls off right now." He pulled at the breech cloth, but never saw his target, for the bullet shattered the top of his head and he went down like a blasted buffalo. Jim turned, his eyes wide, and the second bullet struck his neck, which spurted a fountain of blood. He clutched at his throat, twisted crazily, then fell.

After firing, Fargo spun behind the tree trunk as Lonnie and the bearded man, with time to draw, flung bullets at his firing position; but he was certain they never saw him, they saw just the rustle of tall grass. Then they scuttled for cover behind a great boulder.

There was a long silence while he reloaded and began to work out a strategy for getting behind the men. He came alert at the sound of horses in a sudden scramble. The buffalo men were hightailing west, hidden by boulders, so that he had no target. He smiled. They thought it an Indian ambush—for who else would rescue a redskin?—and they were not hanging around, not after their kind of fun.

Fargo came forward slowly. Although the Indian's black eyes glowed, he didn't speak. Fargo pulled the knife from his boot jacket, looked at the Sioux for a long moment, smiled, then slashed the ropes.

The brave's eyes were intense. He put his right hand over his heart. "Red Sun," he said.

"Fargo." He, too, put his hand over his heart.

A look of simple dignity came to the broad, strong face. "Red Sun would be blood brother to Fargo," he said in Dakota dialect.

Fargo, looking into the glowing black eyes, felt moved. "Fargo is blood brother to Red Sun."

It didn't take long to get ointment and cloth from his saddlebag to put over the chest slashes. The Indian watched with a small smile. He was muscled and powerful, and didn't seem weakened by his blood loss. To endure, whatever the pain, especially in front of the white man—this was the code of the red man. Fargo wondered if the Sioux could read the one-quarter Cherokee in his own blood lines.

After a long silence, the Indian spoke. "Red Sun owes his life to Fargo."

"Fargo likes the courage of Red Sun."

The Sioux's natural expression was stern, and that's how he looked now.

"The white man," he said, "kill many, many buffalo. For the skins. They destroy our food." His eyes burned fiercely.

"These are evil men," said Fargo.

They were sitting opposite each other, cross-legged, Indian-style. Red Sun's experience of white men, Fargo felt, had been nothing but vicious.

The Sioux was silent, then spoke slowly. "The white man is evil. They have the teeth of the wolf. They tear at our food, at our people, at our land." His face was proud and hard-set.

He's young, Fargo thought, and someday he may be a chief. "Not all white men are evil," he said.

The Sioux held his head high, and his face was composed, as if, Fargo thought, he never in his life had experienced a defeat, as if he thought himself invincible. He looked steadily at Fargo.

"The white man and the red man cannot live in peace," he said.

Fargo shook his head. "Red Sun and Fargo are in peace."

The Sioux looked steadily at his face. "Fargo is not as other white men," he said finally.

Later, when the Sioux tried to jump on the back of his pony, he faltered. Because he needed rest and fresh bandages, Fargo decided to bring him back to the campsite. When Sister Catherine and Sister Elizabeth saw Red Sun, their eyes snapped open in shock.

"This is Red Sun," he told them.

Sister Catherine, though uncomfortable, tried to smile. "Mr. Fargo, I hope I'm not hurting his feelings, but may I ask what you're doing?"

"Doing?"

"Doing. We're in a wilderness. And you tell us we are surrounded by dangers. Don't you think you have increased these dangers, bringing this savage into our camp?"

He glanced at Sister Elizabeth, who, for once, did not wear a ready smile.

"First of all, dear sister, this is no savage, this is a Sioux." He smiled grimly. "Second, I wouldn't bring him if I thought him a danger to our trip." He stared at her face, so damned pretty, even though she did a lot of scowling. "When are you going to let me run this outfit?"

She shrugged. "As long as I'm paying you, Fargo, I have a right to say what I think. You can be wrong sometimes." Then she mumbled, "Probably most times."

A ballbuster, he thought.

Red Sun had been watching the interchange with an amused smile. "The squaw," he said in Dakota dialect, "makes sound like wind in a cave."

Fargo laughed.

Sister Catherine looked at the Sioux suspiciously. "Do you understand him? What did he say?"

Red Sun looked at the women, still with his amused smile. "The squaws are like flowers of the sun, but their clothing is like the cloud of the night."

"They are squaws," Fargo said, "who serve only the Great Spirit, and are not meant for the men of the earth."

"For the Great Spirit." Red Sun looked at them impassively. "They are given in sacrifice to the Great Spirit? Are they not too old?"

Fargo smiled. "The white man does not sacrifice the maiden to the Great Spirit. She can serve and live."

"The ways of the white man are strange."

Red Sun looked puzzled, but seemed willing to respect the idea, though his tribal custom must find it curious.

Suddenly, Fargo became aware that one of the sisters was missing.

"Where's Sister Teresa?" he asked abruptly.

"Well, I was about to tell you, but got a bit upset by our Indian guest. She went upstream for a swim. She should have been back by now. I've been worried."

He felt a flash of premonition.

"What troubles Fargo?" the Sioux asked.

"It's the third squaw. She has gone to swim and has been away a long time."

Fargo watched the Sioux move smoothly toward the stream, and, after a glance at Sister Catherine's worried face, he followed. From her prints, Sister Teresa had gone upstream, probably out of modesty, where they found the sign of a struggle, then the heavier print of a horse, carrying a double load.

"It is the ones who kill the buffalo," said Red Sun, pointing to a nicked hoof. He had been tracking these men before.

Fargo nodded. Back at the campsite he gave Sister Catherine the gun taken from Gibson. "We're going after Teresa," he said.

"Where is she?" Sister Catherine's eyes were wide.

"We aim to find that out." He kept his voice casual.

"Was it the Indians?" she demanded.

"No. We won't be long."

She bit her lip, then looked distastefully at the gun. "Will I need this?"

"It's better to have it than not," he said.

Her blue eyes glittered. "Just bring Sister Teresa back."

The trail was easy to follow, and they pushed the horses. Red Sun, bareback on his pony, seemed to have an instinct where the trail went, and at times took short-cuts past trees and boulders and road windings to pick up the trail again. After hard riding, he held up his hand and pointed to a hollow enclosed by boulders.

They tethered the horses and moved quietly forward in a crouch.

Fargo raised his rifle, peering intently through the sight, then lowered it because his arm was quivering; the target was so damned funny. He wondered, in fact, if anyone, sprawled over Sister Teresa, who had been stripped naked, it damn well called for a precision shot.

He looked again at Lonnie's bare butt. Lonnie was sprawled over Sister Teresa, who had been stripped naked. He could see the white of her body and legs under the buffalo man's darker body. She was trying to fight, but it didn't come to much. It had to be out of fear for her life. The bearded man, Sam, nearby, watched with a lustful grin.

Fargo aimed carefully. It surely would be a nightmare to a virgin nun to find her violator suddenly dead on top of her. No, he had to nick Lonnie's tail; that should put a quick freeze on his heat. Delicately, he squeezed the trig-ger. The bark of the rifle and Lonnie's leap into the air seemed to happen at the same time. Lonnie then clapped his hand to his butt and yelled. The bearded man, Sam, standing as a fascinated spectator, jumped, and pulled his gun, but Fargo's next shot knocked it out of his hand. Sam shook his arm in pain, but slowly raised both hands.

Lonnie kept swearing, obviously not seriously hurt, and pulled the jeans at his feet up to cover himself. But Sister Teresa still lay there, stunned.

Fargo came forward, his rifle held low, finger on the trigger. "Got a sore butt, Lonnie?" His tone was sarcastic.

Lonnie stared at him, astonished, no doubt, that this stranger who had shot at his tail with such amazing aim also knew his name. He had a bullet head, a cruel mouth, a thick, muscular body.

And when Red Sun came out, his face grim, tomahawk in hand, Lonnie's eyes screwed tight. He pulled at his jeans, in obvious pain from the nick in his buttocks.

"Throw the gun, and be very careful," Fargo said.

Lonnie threw the gun. He did not look at Red Sun.

"Who are you?"

"The name is Fargo."

Sister Teresa, he noticed, chose to ignore him, and walked to where her garment lay. She slipped it over her full breasts and womanly hips.

"Is this redskin with you?" Lonnie asked, still not looking at Red Sun.

Fargo dug his finger in his ear. This stinking hyena had balls. He should be dead by this time for the games he had played with Sister Teresa and with Red Sun, but he was talking bold as brass.

"I don't know what kind of a white man you are," Lonnie was saying, "but you gotta know what these murdering Sioux are doing to our people."

Our people! Fargo smiled grimly. "Everyone's doing some murdering. And some are doing raping."

Sister Teresa, by this time fully clothed, stood off to the side, watching, but he couldn't see her expression.

"Listen, Fargo," Lonnie said reasonably. "We didn't know this woman belonged to anyone. Didn't even know she was a church woman. We came to the stream to water our horses, and we see a beauty, all alone, bathing. What would you expect from any hungry man out on the trail for two months?"

Fargo rubbed his chin. In a way, he thought, Lonnie made a good case. A nude woman like Teresa with those big breasts, romping in the river out here in the wild, had to be more than the flesh of man could stand. It was a bit of bad luck that brought them together. What now? He couldn't shoot them down in cold blood, though, if the situation had been the other way, a skunk like Lonnie wouldn't think twice.

He looked at Red Sun.

"Kill him," the Sioux said.

"Fargo does not shoot a man without a gun," he said.

The Sioux's face went dark with anger. "He has taken the squaw. He has killed many buffalo. He should die."

But Fargo couldn't do it. And what about Sister Teresa, who had just gone through a hell of a time? Was she now to see a cold-blooded killing?

"No, it can't be done. We must get the rifles from the horses."

Red Sun stared, and it was not hard to tell what was passing through his mind. He thought Fargo was acting like a fool, but he would not block him because Fargo had saved his life.

Red Sun moved swiftly to the horses and pulled the big rifles from their saddle holsters.

Lonnie had paid no attention to the interchange between Fargo and the Indian, preoccupied by the pain in his butt, and aware that someone like Fargo would not shoot an unarmed man, especially in front of a woman.

"I don't want to see your stinking carcass again," Fargo commanded. "Get going."

Lonnie looked at Sister Teresa and licked his lips.

Fargo's gun barked and kicked dirt at Lonnie's feet, which catapulted him and Sam into action, and within minutes their horses were off down the trail.

Red Sun looked at him with hard eyes. "Red Sun would not treat his enemies like this."

"No, I reckon not," said Fargo.

Red Sun's eyes were hard. "The enemy you do not kill will come back to kill you."

Fargo said nothing. The Indian had a simple code of justice: The enemy must die. And in a territory like this, where it was kill or be killed, the code seemed to work. The white man, however, was bred to a code with compassion in it. But a man like Lonnie was white—would he have compassion?

Red Sun was looking at him with a strange smile.

"Why does Red Sun smile?"

"Fargo is a mighty warrior. But he is soft. It is a great danger to be soft." He waved his hand in a slow semicircle. "All this land belongs to the Sioux. Because the Sioux too are warriors. They do not have the softness."

Fargo nodded solemnly. He understood the Indian. He was saying it was fatal to be soft, and if the white man was cursed with softness, he would never triumph over the red man, who was merciless to his enemy.

Red Sun continued to look at him, and Fargo waited until he spoke again. "If these men had been Sioux, you would have killed," he said, and turned away as Sister Teresa came up. Her face was inscrutable.

"I would not have objected if you had killed them," she said.

He stared hard at her. "I try not to kill in cold blood. And you were partly at fault for swimming nude. The men out here are not exactly studying for the church."

She shrugged. "Anyway, thank you, Mr. Fargo."

She sounded low-spirited, and, of course, she should be.

"Were you hurt?" he asked.

"No." Then she looked at him. "Not at all."

"Not at all? What does that mean?"

Her clean brown eyes glittered. "I think it means not at all."

He stared at her, then at Red Sun standing still, holding a rifle in each hand.

How'd you explain a woman like this? he wondered. All tangled up with a coyote like Lonnie, and still not complaining. She either was a saint, or something else. Well, he thought, watching Red Sun go off for the horses, a woman didn't necessarily stamp out her natural instincts just because she put on the cloth of a nun.

When Red Sun rode up, leading his pinto, he said to Sister Teresa, "You ride with me." And on the way back he tried to fix in his mind that she was a special woman, dedicated to the life of the spirit, and not an ordinary female, as her body jostling against his kept telling him.

As they neared camp, the Sioux came up. "Red Sun must now leave Fargo." His face was proud but remote.

Fargo put his hand over his heart. "Fargo wishes peace to Red Sun."

The Sioux is angry, he thought as he watched Red Sun ride off.

When Sister Catherine, after a few discreet questions, found out what had happened, she turned pale.

"I told you, Sister Teresa, to swim nearby, where we could see you." Her voice was stern.

Sister Teresa just shrugged.

"You don't seem to care much, do you?" Sister Catherine persisted.

"Please don't make a fuss," Sister Teresa said, scowling.

"Why do such things happen to you?"

"May I point out that it happened to you, too," Sister Teresa flashed back.

The blue eyes sparked. "I didn't go out asking for it."

"Oh, don't bother me."

Sister Catherine's face flamed. "You may not care two pins what happens to you, but you have no right to endanger the rest of us. This brute would have forced you to tell where you were going, who you were with, how much money we have. Don't you see?"

Sister Teresa bit her lip. "I'm sorry. But I'd like you to keep in mind that I didn't go for a swim with the *hope* of being raped."

Sister Catherine looked startled. "No, I don't suppose you did. But I ask you to just stick close to us. Don't wander around. That's all."

Fargo had listened to the interchange with a touch of amusement. Sister Teresa, he thought, might be a nun outside, but on the inside she seemed to have a touch of the devil.

6

The terrain, for a time, became rolling flatlands with yellow wheat grass glinting in the sun; then it became wooded with sturdy oaks and leafy maples. He could always see, on his right, the shoulder of the mountain with its pitted crags and peaks and level slabs of solid rock. Sister Catherine chafed at their slow movement through the wooded area.

"Mr. Fargo, at this pace we'll be a year older by the time we reach Aberdeen."

"At least you'll be alive," he said. She was always sniping, it seemed to him. What the hell was biting her?

That night, after dinner, she said again, "I think you are extra-cautious, Mr. Fargo. You seem to think there's an Indian hiding behind every rock."

"That's how I survive." She had no idea, in spite of her experience, of the violence that lurked in this land. Though she sniped at him a lot, dammit, she was one beautiful woman. In spite of a strong effort to control it, the image of her full-formed womanly body, when Gibson had her nude, often slipped into his mind. He would grit his teeth; it might have been the heat of the sun and hunger of his flesh that put such pictures in his head. It was damned distracting, and he wondered if this blurred his concentration on the dangers of the trail.

The moon was a big silver ball in the sky when he fell asleep, and because his feelings were erotic, he was in the middle of a sensual dream in which Tess and he were doing a number of very nice things, when he felt the cold iron muzzle of a gun against his forehead.

"Just hold still, Fargo, and I'll let you live a few minutes more."

His eyes shot open, but he knew Lonnie's voice. He felt goose pimples all over his body.

Lonnie reached over to his holster, pulled the Colt, and tossed it into the brush. The smell of sweat and smoked buffalo meat oozed from Lonnie's burly bulk.

"Now get up, slow, and I mean slow. I've got an itchy trigger finger. Turn around. Put your hands behind your back." His voice was soft.

Fargo felt the rope go tightly around his wrists, double-knotted. It was one hell of a setup.

Now Lonnie moved in front of him, and in the brilliant moonlight his mouth was twisted in a cruel smile.

"Well, look at Fargo, all trussed up like a hog for killing. You don't look so big now, *Mr.* Fargo, do you?"

Fargo cleared his throat. "Where'd you get the gun?"

Lonnie's grin widened. "The gun? I got it in my saddlebag. Your stupid redskin never bothered to look. Sit down." Lonnie himself sat cross-legged and rubbed his backside tenderly. "I've been tailing you for hours, Fargo. A lot of time to think about you." He stopped and waited. "Don't you want to know why?"

Fargo looked into the cold eyes. "I think you're going to tell me."

Lonnie nodded. "Oh, yeah, sure. I can't keep this to myself. I'm sorry Sam isn't here to enjoy this. He didn't want to tangle with you. I was thinking what a great sense of fun you have." He grinned, his face really evil. "It takes a big sense of fun to shoot a man in the ass while he's screwing." He leaned back. "I'll tell you, real honest, Fargo, that if it wasn't *my* ass, I'd get a big laugh outa it. A big laugh. But it was my ass, and I won't sit easy for a month." He glanced toward the wagon, about fifty feet away, under the shelter of the oaks. If only, Fargo hoped, one of the sisters would shoot Lonnie's head off.

Lonnie was watching him. "Old Stoneface. Well, I know you sympathize with me, but don't care to show it." He hitched his belt. "You sit here. Something tells me there's a nice prize waiting there, in that wagon." He stroked his chin, and his tone became pleasant. "I know that redskin wanted to kill me. I don't blame him. And I thought it mighty stupid of you not to listen to him. That's why I'm going to do you a favor. Then I'm going to take good care of you. You'll see." His voice went hard. "Lonnie Starr don't like to look ridiculous."

Fargo, looking into the shallow brown eyes, could see a cold killer. And he had all the aces. All. After a moment, Lonnie spoke again. "I gotta say it, Fargo, you got balls. Now, you just relax while I take care of a few things."

He crept quietly to the wagon, and it didn't take long before Fargo heard the voices, screeches, thumps.

Fargo heard the sounds and twisted his wrists, trying desperately to loosen the cords, which just tightened as he struggled. Then he stared at the moon, because it hurt too much to listen to the sounds that came from the wagon. They were all in this hellhole because, like an idiot, he had yielded to the lunatic idea of letting a man like Lonnie live. His stupid idea of not shooting a man in cold blood. By the same logic that you shot a rattler, you oughta shoot a man like Lonnie.

Then the sisters came out, their hands tied with rope. They all wore their sleeping clothes, linen bodices and knee-length pantaloons that fit tightly. Sister Catherine's golden hair fell to her shoulders and glowed in the moonlight. Her face was grim, more with anger than fear, he thought. She stared at him, trussed up, and the look she gave him seared his gut. Sister Elizabeth looked fearful. Sister Teresa seemed to have done some trick in her head, for she did not look discomposed.

Lonnie came up close. "Hey, Fargo, I went fishing, and look what I caught. Three beauties. Three." He came in front of Fargo, stared at him for a long time, then spoke in an icy voice. "You skinned my butt, Fargo, right in the middle of something good. So this is what I'm gonna do. I'm goin' on from where you interrupted, with this honey girl here." He pointed to Teresa. "After that, I'm gonna string you up on that tree there. A feast for the buzzards. Figure you'll last two days. Then I'm gonna travel with these beauties, and we'll all have a big time together. How do you like that, Fargo?"

Fargo just looked at him.

Lonnie's face was grim. "You don't like it? Well, I don't blame you. Not a nice way to go. But you're not lucky." He turned to look at Sister Teresa. "Now, I'm lucky. Look at what I'm gonna play with."

Sister Catherine spoke then, her voice blistering with contempt. "What kind of a man are you? You don't even sound like a man. You sound more like some animal."

There was a dead moment, then Lonnie looked around him. "Are you talking to me, lady?" His voice was cold.

"Yes, you."

Lonnie stared at her, and his face went red. He moved quick as a panther, grabbed her, pulled down her pantaloons, exposing her buttocks. And he began to spank her. She twisted and writhed, but he was burly and strong and he held her fixed. Fargo, watching, could hear the thump of his palm against her white buttocks, which soon turned red from the repeated assault.

At first she wriggled, then she screeched, then she yelled, then she went silent.

Fargo could do nothing but groan inside. His wrists behind him were raw from trying to loosen the rope, tied with tight, unbreakable knots. Again he cursed himself for not blasting this dog. He had made the one unforgivable oversight, not checking Lonnie's saddlebag for weapons.

After Sister Catherine went silent, Lonnie stopped the spanking, as if he got no kicks unless his victim made noise.

He turned to Fargo. "She's got a terrific rump, Fargo. Ain't it a pity you won't ever get a piece of it." Then he looked at Sister Teresa, his mouth in a leer. "But there's a fine hunk of flesh. And since you ain't got much of a future, Fargo, I'm gonna give you the pleasure of watching a top gun working his woman."

He pulled Teresa forward by her roped hands. Then with a quick movement he pulled at her pantaloons and her bodice, and she was on the earth stark naked, her body shocking white under the bright glow of the moon. Her breasts were heavy, her hips full, her stomach flat, and the red hair of her head was replayed on the triangle between her thighs. "Look, Fargo, just look. Ever see so much woman? Well, I'm gonna give you something to think about while you're hanging on that tree with the buzzards picking at your liver." He grinned and pulled off his checked shirt, then his boots, then his jeans. He had black matted hair on his chest, and hair on his thick, muscular legs. He looked down at his thick sexual arousal, grinned at Fargo, and stepped toward Teresa. Then the first shot boomed. It ripped part of his left shoulder, and the second ripped his right shoulder, and he flipped back like a toy doll. As he started to fall, the third bullet hit his groin, spinning him forward, and the fourth bullet ripped away part of his skull.

The women screamed and screamed, and then there was silence.

Red Sun moved noiselessly on his moccasins and looked down at Lonnie's hacked body gushing blood. Then Red Sun looked at Sister Teresa on the ground; his face was impassive. Then he came to Fargo. His knife flashed in the moonlight, and Fargo drew a deep breath and rubbed his wrists, which were practically numb.

The big Sioux spoke slowly. "Now, Red Sun owes nothing to Fargo."

7

The wagon trundled behind him, and they made good headway on the trail. It was a beautiful summer day with cotton clouds floating against a polished blue sky. The air was so clear that he could see, almost without strain, details of the sculptured peaks of the mountain. Yellow wheat grass went out in waves to the left. Up high, a hawk circled lazily looking for lunch.

A good day to be alive, Fargo thought, and the pinto, more than once, without reason, pranced as if it felt glad to be strong and feel the earth against its hooves. Even Sister Catherine, for the time being, stopped her potshots at him, probably because of the peaceful terrain.

But Fargo did not lose his concentration. He had let it happen once, which would have been fatal but for Red Sun. The Indian had slipped away as mysteriously as he had appeared. He didn't stick around to remind Fargo again that the enemy you didn't kill would come back to kill you. Red Sun had just put his hand over his heart, looked with brotherly feeling into Fargo's eyes, then slipped away.

As he scanned the horizons from the back of the trotting pinto, Fargo thought about Red Sun. The Sioux was a solo figure, strong, unafraid, who rode the territory like a free spirit. He took pleasure in the world of trees and streams, the mountains and the eagles. And into his world had come the white man with his fire stick and great talent of killing, and pushing, pushing the Sioux. Could he make peace with that?

Fargo felt a powerful sense of kinship with Red Sun. Perhaps only the accident of their skin color made them different, for under that, he felt, they were two of a kind.

The little party traveled on without incident, stopping

only to eat, to feed and water the horses. Before nightfall, he found a sheltering overhang of rock near a sparkling stream. The sisters bathed and washed their garments, and he, too, dived in to clean off his sweat and dirt.

Sitting around the small fire at night, Sister Catherine said, "Things are quiet, Mr. Fargo. Perhaps we can reach Aberdeen without any more bloodshed."

"Let's hope so." He smiled. They were actually passing through a nest of hornets, but he understood her wanting it nice and quiet. She looked fresh and clear-eyed from her swim in the stream.

"I think," she said, "we should *try* to *avoid* trouble."

He glanced at her. "We don't go looking for trouble, sister. It finds us."

"I'm not sure of that, Mr. Fargo." Her lips were pressed.

He looked at her through slitted eyes.

"It all started, Mr. Fargo, you may remember, because of the Indian. You helped him. Very nice, of course—but if we had minded our own business, we would have avoided the whole mess."

He scowled. She was the damnedest woman, always slicing up things and turning him wrong. "I do what I have to do," he said grimly. "I moved to clear the trail."

Sister Teresa folded her hands over her cowl. "I think, sister, you're being unfair to Mr. Fargo. I hate to think what would have happened if not for him." She shut her eyes. "Vile men abusing me."

"You don't have to be so picturesque in your languge, Sister Teresa!"

"But I agree," said Sister Elizabeth, her fine black eyes flashing. "How terrible—to be at the mercy of such a man. You yourself called him an animal."

"He was an animal," Sister Catherine said, "and he died terribly. Yet he was a human being." Fargo saw a glimpse of mockery in her eyes. She's going to needle me, he thought.

He smiled. "Men out here are starved for women. And the sight of a nude woman brings out the beast in a man."

There was a long silence.

"Is there a beast in every man?" asked Sister Teresa.

"We are all as nature made us," Fargo said.

Sister Catherine frowned. "God has given us the spirit to master our animal desires. Let us not forget that, Mr. Fargo." Then, with a strange smile, she added, "I just don't understand how he managed to tie you up like that. You're supposed to be the best in the territory, according to the blacksmith in Devil's Corner."

She obviously liked to needle him, and that was that. "It proves that anyone can make a mistake," he said. Actually, Red Sun had made the mistake, by not checking the saddlebags for weapons. But Fargo took the blame for it. She had touched a sore spot. Curiously, the image that jumped into his mind was her white buttocks getting spanked. Lonnie, damn his soul to hell, hadn't exaggerated when he'd said Sister Catherine had one great rump. He felt an urge at the moment to spank her for sniping at him. But he had to shut out such pictures and concentrate instead on the dangers that filled the territory.

"I'm afraid," she said, "that we can't afford any mistakes."

She was right—one misstep could be fatal.

"Time for shut-eye." He stood up. "We'll get up early and move fast, while things are still quiet."

It was a good night for sleeping. A cool east wind brought the clean scent of wheat grass; a golden moon, rising late, threw a mysterious look over the stone crags, casting long shadows.

His bed site under a tree was about two hundred feet from the wagon, and he could still hear the low voices of the women. After they went silent, he picked up the tumbling sound of the stream. He shut his eyes, and as he sank into sleep, the picture of Sister Teresa, as he had seen her yesterday, with white body and heavy breasts, flashed on the screen of his mind. He was not yet asleep, and he groaned, aware that his body fiercely craved a woman, and that he was living day to day in a vise between temptation and prohibition. Because of circumstances, he had seen the nude bodies of both Sister Catherine and Sister Teresa, and it did nothing to quiet the urges of his flesh. And yet the sisters wore cloth that made them untouchable.

He looked up at the shadowed crags. It was one hell of

a setup, but he'd grit his teeth and bear it. What else could he do? At Aberdeen, if they ever reached it, he would pitch a big one, he promised himself.

He sighed, then drifted off to sleep.

The sound was slight, just pressure on a leaf, but it went deep into his sleeping brain, and touched the alarm, and his body mobilized. The sound was different, not the cry of a bird, bubble of a stream, scuttle of a small animal, the kind his mind interpreted as the safe sounds of night. His eyes clicked open, and the night was all around, the silver of the moon glinting off the leaves of the tree over him. The sound again, the soft crunch on a twig, and his mind instantly eased. No Indian would make such a mistake. And the sound was light: his mind clicked off the possibilities, and they were strange. One of the sisters, suddenly gone loco, tiptoeing toward him with a weapon? His eyes shifted to the right.

A woman, all right, in white pantaloons, trying to be light-footed. A tilt of his head brought her into view. But she was clearly empty-handed: Sister Teresa.

He watched her move. It took ten steps before she became aware he was watching. She looked startled, stopped, smiled, and came forward.

"I was hoping to reach here and be the one to wake you."

"That'll be the day," he said. "How would you do that?"

"With a kiss." She stood boldly in front of him.

He stared. Apparently her rough time with Lonnie had snapped something; she was forgetting she was a nun. But her body, with her big, round breasts and womanly hips, made him fully aware she was a woman as well as a nun.

And considering the way he had been feeling, this was a rotten trick to play on him now. He felt a sting of anger. Why, with all the things on his mind, did he have to wrestle with this?

"I think you're sleepwalking, Sister Teresa. You'd better get back to the wagon."

She smiled, pinched her arm. "No, I don't think I'm sleepwalking." She sat down alongside him. "I'm very much awake. I wanted to thank you for your help. You were so brave and strong." She looked at his body, bare to the waist. "And so handsome."

God, this was going to be a problem. Sister Teresa, out of her head, with lusts of the flesh all over her, and he horny as a mountain goat in heat.

"Listen, Sister Teresa, I'm only a man, and the flesh is weak. You're tying me in all sorts of knots. Now, be a good girl and hightail back to the wagon."

"But I want to stay here with you. To show my gratitude." She pulled at her bodice, and her heavy breasts fell out, round, with pink nipples already erect.

Oh God, he thought, feeling his flesh begin to crawl. He took two deep breaths. She was out of her mind, and he had to control himself, blast her ass, or everything would fall apart.

"Sister Teresa," he said sternly, "what you're doing is really unfair. You're tempting a starving man. I want you to put that damned thing on and get the hell out of here, right now."

She looked at him a bit uncertainly.

"Don't you like me?" she asked plaintively.

"Like you?" he raged. "For Christ's sake, you're a nun! Have you forgotten that? Even for what you have already done, you'll hate yourself in the morning. You're a nun, Sister Teresa, a nun!"

She started to rise, and he thought at last he had reached her, that reason had returned, but instead, she started to pull down her pantaloons, and his shocked eyes looked at the top of her white flat belly, firmly rounded thighs. He rose to his feet, petrified.

"I'm not a nun," she said quietly.

The words didn't quite make sense.

"No, Mr. Fargo, not a nun. None of us are nuns. Actually, we're teachers."

He stared uncomprehending.

"Yes." She smiled. "We're teachers on our way to Aberdeen, to teach there under the supervision of Sister Catherine, who's really just Cathy Brown. We were advised to dress as nuns, to masquerade, because this is dangerous territory, and the men are wicked." She sighed. "They certainly are that, Mr. Fargo." She looked at him, standing in his shorts, with muscular chest, slender waist, powerful trunk and legs, and the great, virile bunch-up in his shorts. "I'm trying to bring out the wickedness in you, Mr. Fargo, but you're putting up a terrible fight."

His mind had begun to grapple with the sense of what she had said, that the three were not sisters at all, but teachers, for God's sake, and all this time he had wrapped them in halos, put them beyond reach. Schoolmarms! He was tempted to burst out laughing, and then he thought of Sister Catherine, now just plain Cathy Brown, damn her, who had been shooting all that spiritual stuff at him. What a job she'd done! Masquerade! By God, she did one sweet job of hokum.

"Then all this time, Sister Catherine—I mean, Cathy Brown—was just putting on an act?"

Teresa nodded, looked strangely at him a moment, then slipped off her pantaloons completely. She had nice full hips, a lovely white belly, and tempting maidenhair at her triangle.

"Cathy," she said, "has been a novice. She almost went the whole way, but withdrew at the last moment." Teresa smiled. "Like the rest of us, she couldn't smother her womanly desires." She paused. "I'm disappointed in you, Fargo."

"What?" He stared at her, brought back with a shock from the whirl of his thoughts to the fact that in front of him was one honey of a woman, entirely nude, and no longer untouchable.

She was looking at him strangely. "I remember you saying a nude woman brought out the beast in a man. I see no beast here."

His eyes squinted hard at her for almost a full minute, then he dropped his shorts.

"Do you see one now?" he asked.

All his bottled desires had surged into his maleness, and the thrust of him looked ferocious. Teresa's eyes went wide almost with shock, and then they glittered.

When he grabbed her, she put up her mouth up for kissing. She had sensual thick lips, and they clung to his own. His hand went to her breasts, creamy as silk and firm and round. Her nipples pouted, now erect with passion. His mouth dropped to taste one, and his tongue flicked skillfully over the swollen nipple. His hands moved over her other breast, then down over her back to her silken, tight buttocks. He found the beautifully shaped mounds and kneaded them with pleasure. Then his finger went between her thighs and entered the juicy warmth there, touched her sensitivity, and she groaned out with passion. He stroked her until her body went taut, and she groaned again. Then she sank to her knees, and her mouth reached for his maleness with wolfish hunger, and he watched, amazed at her intensity. She kept at it, licking and engulfing, insatiable, until finally he gently pushed her back to the earth, where he spread her soft thighs, entered her easily, feeling the juicy warmth instantly surround him. As he moved within her, now totally, her eyes became glazed, like a woman in a dream.

He grasped her creamy smooth butt again and began his fast movements; she murmured with intense pleasure, and her body arched in rhythm, and went higher and higher, and during his thrusting he became aware how much his animal desire had been bottled up, feeling the tension increase with his thrusts. Then he withdrew, turned her over, pierced her buttocks, and again went deep into her, feeling the impact of her voluptuous mounds. His hands from behind grasped her breasts, and the pleasure kept sharpening, while every so often she would tighten as if she were experiencing intolerable pleasure, and then finally he felt it, the huge swelling that filled her, made her gasp, and when his climax came, she moaned as if ecstasy had turned to pain. He felt great pulsations, one after the other, and held her silky flesh until, finally, after the tension drained out of him, he let go and pulled away.

There was, he could tell, a new mood in the camp at breakfast, and it had to do not only with his discovery that the women were teachers and not nuns, which stripped them of halos, but with the air that crackled between Catherine and Teresa. More than once Catherine threw a hard shot at Teresa, who, however, took it sweetly, as if nothing, this special morning, could disturb her disposition.

It made him smile; nothing sweetened a woman more than a good and heavy roll in the hay. For that matter, he too felt damned good. A rip-roaring hunk of sex, he decided, was the best thing ever invented for a man or a woman.

It was a fine June day, and they made mileage without mishap until, on a quick scouting trip into a wooded area, which always posed the threat of ambush, he picked up a faint print about two days old of an unshod pony. And not Red Sun's, for the print had a different hoof marking, a heavier lean to the left. He followed it, carefully checking the movement, its stop and go, and judged it the scout of a larger group. He remembered that Phelps, the barman at Twin Oak, had talked of a Sioux hunting party. This far south, he speculated, it might be a war party, which would mean trouble. Still, it was not a fresh print, and therefore nothing urgent. Miles to the east, he knew of a trail used frequently by settlers as they pushed west, Hell's Crossing, a trail that more than once had exploded in attacks by Sioux on the wagons. He decided that for the time being, they had nothing to fear from a party of young bucks out to raise hell.

He knocked off a well-fleshed rabbit hopping near a bush, then put the pinto into a canter and picked up the wagon as it trundled south. Catherine, he noticed, fixed a sharp eye on him.

"Trouble, Mr. Fargo?" He'd been away too long.

"No, no trouble," he said cheerfully. "Just checking the trail. I picked up a rabbit for lunch." What could be more unwise than telling three women that a Sioux war party might be prowling the area?

They didn't stop for lunch until early afternoon, to build sharp appetites for the rabbit, which was skinned and pan-fried, and again seasoned by Catherine with herbs she had found along the trail.

They sat around the fire, and the taste of fresh coffee from the pot gave him a pleasant lift. He looked at Catherine, and each time she looked back at him boldly, as if she had nothing on her conscience.

"Well," he said, "this is good coffee. You make a fine cup of coffee, *Sister* Catherine." And he smiled meaningfully. It was the first time he had brought himself to use her name, and something had crept into his accent on "Sister."

She studied him coolly. "I'm well aware, Mr. Fargo, that you know by now from Teresa that we are teachers and not nuns. Well, it was not my intention to deceive you, but we had been strictly instructed by the principal of our school, the man who hired us, to use this camouflage. Otherwise, he said, he couldn't vouch for our safety in such an untamed territory. Teresa has let the cat out of the bag, and I won't inquire into the reasons. I'm sure she had them. We are all adults here, and in certain matters, responsible only to ourselves. I'm trying hard not to judge Teresa, but I think she has, in some way, increased the risks in our travel."

She was, he was thinking, one lady with balls. He had expected to have her on the ropes, defending herself because of all the pious bullshit she had put out, but she just came out slugging.

"What risks?" he asked.

"Don't you think it obvious, Mr. Fargo?"

"No, I don't."

She looked at the other two women, and they in turn looked at her with serious faces.

"Before this, we were three nuns with a protector. Now we are three women with a man. I'm sure you see the difference."

He smiled. "Yes, there is a difference."

"Before this," she said acidly, "you could concentrate on your job—which is to bring us safely to Aberdeen. I wonder if you have lost this concentration. Perhaps you have other things in mind."

She was one dilly of a dame, he thought, all stiff and starched, with iron up her tail.

"I don't think I'm gonna lose my concentration because you're teachers and not nuns. I intend to get you safely to Aberdeen."

She threw a withering look at Teresa. "Let us hope, Mr. Fargo, that you can keep your mind on the job."

He rubbed his chin instead of giving expression to a stifled impulse to whip her butt. "You know," he said, his tone sarcastic, "you did some great job of impersonating a nun. I never heard more hallelujah hogwash than came outa you. I particularly like that one about God gave us spirit to master our animal desires. How'd you keep a straight face putting out that spiel, huh, *Sister* Catherine?"

Her lips went tight, and her tone silky. "Thank you, Mr. Fargo. One can see you're a gentleman clear through. I'd like you to know that though I'm not a nun, most of what I said in a religious vein I believe. I almost did become a nun, just for your information."

He looked at her face, beautiful in anger, but he remembered her body, her rounded hips, her golden hair, shapely legs. "But you discovered you were more woman than nun, is that what happened?"

Her eyes blazed at him. "If it was, Mr. Fargo, it's none of your business. Your business is to get us to Aberdeen as quick as you can."

"Yes, Miss Catherine, ma'am," he said sarcastically and glanced at the others. Teresa was looking at him strangely, and Elizabeth was puzzled and serious.

He didn't like the way he was feeling, and he stood up. "Aberdeen won't get any closer until the wheels of that wagon start turning. Let's go."

He put the pinto into a slow jog, and they went through the wooded area without incident. His eyes looked for clues, the telltale marks of man and animal, but his mind circled on the women. That damned Catherine, for example, had a lot of iron in her, spirit and spunk. She had more spirit than good sense, and that could be trouble. The way she had sassed Lonnie, a sadist bastard if he ever saw one, and God knew what damage he would have done if Red Sun hadn't happened. Where in hell had Red Sun gone, anyway? He was a master tracker, and the territory belonged to him and his kind. Red Sun had really been a blood brother. Fargo's teeth gritted. He'd be buzzard meat right now if not for Red Sun.

They were now on rising ground and only a mile from Hell's Crossing, where the settler trail from the east joined their trail, which meandered southwest.

He restlessly scanned the horizon, the great rocks to his right shouldering its way south, the great spread of wooded land to his left, and the thicket of bushes to his front. Behind him, almost half a mile, still out of sight, the wagon trundled along. Then he felt the sudden tick of tension; his instinct had picked up a signal. His whole

68

body mobilized with the lightning speed which had always given him, at least in the past, the edge. And at the slight quiver of the bush to his left his gun exploded. The sound in the brush was quiet, almost a whisper. He was off the pinto, rolling, in an instant, into a crouch, frozen, listening, looking. There was deadly silence, too silent. Noiselessly, he reached for the rock at his foot, tossed it to the left of the thicket, and then he saw a Sioux, ferocious war paint on his face, knife in hand, in a killing rush. The Sioux took two steps toward the sound before he realized his mistake, and by that time the bullet had exploded in his brain, stopping further thought. He fell heavily and lay without movement. Fargo moved closer to look at him. His shoulder had been shattered by the first shot, making his bow useless. He was a young brave with a strong body, and Fargo had to admire the guts that let him take a bullet without an outcry.

He dragged the body into the bushes so the women would not see it when the wagon came by. Then he picked up the track of the Sioux, which went eastward. The Indian was a scout, that was clear, one of a war party. Fargo would have to track him; that was unavoidable. He found the Sioux's pony and turned it loose, then wheeled the pinto and cantered back to the wagon. The women had heard the shots, and their faces were serious.

"A coyote in the brush," he said cheerfully. He continued to talk in a casual tone. "We're coming to Hell's Crossing. Settlers from the East use it."

"Why do they call it Hell's Crossing?" asked Catherine.

"Because they catch hell there," he said grimly. "I'll want to scout a little to be sure it's all right to move into. I'll be gone an hour. Meanwhile, it's always smart to keep your guns handy."

Catherine took a breath. "I have this to say for our trip to Aberdeen, Mr. Fargo: It's never dull."

He smiled thinly. "You've got a bad memory. You may remember that back in town, I told you to wait for the cavalry. The trip might have been easier on your nerves."

"Yes, easier," she said, then smiled. "But it might have been dull. Are you expecting trouble?"

"I always expect trouble," he said.

"Just don't go looking for it."

He swung the pinto about. If he looked for it, it was to take it out, so they could move, he thought, but it was hopeless to tell her that. She had some weird ideas about him, and it was easy to see he couldn't change them.

He spurred the pinto, and soon picked up the dead Indian's trail, working it almost half an hour before he picked up tracks of four unshod ponies. He stayed with them until he reached a site where the Sioux had camped. There were smears of red on the grass, crushed berries, dye they used for war paint. It was a war party, all right, for they moved, war-style, in single file. Another half hour of tracking brought him to a crossing where the tracks of two wagons, only a day old, intercepted with the tracks of the Sioux. His jaw firmed as he reined up the pinto. There was small doubt in his mind what he would find up the trail; he'd seen it before. He wheeled the pinto about, to rejoin the wagon.

That night he dug a deeper pit for their fire to keep the light hidden, and after dinner he stayed alert for a long time to sound and sight, not easy under a sickle moon.

He had actually no reason to expect trouble, not yet, but there was plenty to think about what they might find tomorrow. The women picked up his serious mood, and were not playful in talk.

Teresa, though she smiled at him, seemed to understand something was heavy in the air, that it was no time to throw a sex pitch.

After breakfast, when he strapped on an extra gun and checked his boot knife, Catherine's mouth tightened and her eyes fixed on his for a long moment. He wondered what thoughts danced in her head, but he suspected, whatever happened, she'd probably not lose her nerve.

After they reached Hell's Crossing, a junction where the settler wagons from the East turned southwest, he began to move erratically, sometimes traveling with the wagon, sometimes falling behind, sometimes moving far in front. He used all his trailsmanship, instinctively aware the Sioux in this terrain were themselves great masters of the trail. To relax for a minute could mean death.

Then in the late afternoon he saw the birds circling, and his jaw tightened. They circled low, about five, big-bodied birds with their great wingspan. He rode back and stayed close to the wagon. Catherine was scowling.

"What is all that, Mr. Fargo? A dead horse, do you suppose?"

"I don't think we can bypass it. It's right on our trail." Chances were, he thought, the ambush had happened in a narrow strip of the trail.

"But what is it?" she persisted.

"A couple of wagons—busted." He had to be honest; they couldn't be shielded from it.

"What do you mean?"

"I mean it's probably an ambush."

"Ambush? Would you mind explaining, please?"

"It means this is dangerous territory." Could he tell them it most probably would be a massacre? Settlers were not experienced trail fighters; they had no army protection. It was a dead cinch that he'd find a rough party.

Catherine's eyes were steady. "A massacre, is that what you mean, Mr. Fargo?"

His eyes fixed on hers. She looked steady, but didn't like the idea.

"I won't know till we get there." He trotted the pinto alongside the wagon. Elizabeth and Teresa looked serious.

"How do you know it's safe now, Mr. Fargo?"

"Nothing is sure, but I think so. They don't stick around after a raid. They avoid the cavalry. It all happened yesterday."

"Are we going through, then?"

He smiled. "There's no other way. I'll ride up ahead, just a bit. Keep you in sight."

"Is he going to leave us, Catherine?" asked Elizabeth.

Catherine frowned, "Mr. Fargo says there's nothing for us to worry about. I think, by this time, we may believe Mr. Fargo. So grit your teeth, girls. This is rough country, as we've been told over and over."

He smiled. "That's it—now you've got it."

He cantered ahead, and within ten minutes reached a narrowing of the trail, an excellent site for the ambush. As he expected, the area was quiet, except for the buzzards, which he drove off by swinging his rifle, aware of the unwisdom of firing a shot.

It was a massacre, all right. He walked about slowly.

The smell of burned canvas was still in the air. The Sioux had fired flaming arrows at the wagons, forcing the settlers into the open, where the men, three of them, had been picked off by arrows.

One man with a beard, about forty, lay sprawled near a wheel, three arrows in his chest, his eyes shocked open. Scalped. A second man lay on his face, scalped; a third was near the second wagon, his body against the wheel, dead minutes after hitting the ground from a barrage of arrows. Then the women, two of them in their thirties, their dresses over their heads, the smear of blood on their thighs. Two teenage boys, both blond, probably brothers, tomahawked.

Scalping, rape, and slaughter, and the rifles were gone, which made the Sioux even more dangerous. The horses gone, too. The tracks of the moccasins were clear as daylight. Four braves, young, wild, brutal. A broken jug of whiskey smashed against the wheel. It established they had pitched a real drunk while they amused themselves with the women.

His jaw went hard. They were out in front of him somewhere, and he'd have to do something to move forward. They stood in his way.

He'd have to find them before they found him.

Behind him, the wagon had come up and stopped. The women looked and looked—there was nothing he could do. Finally, Catherine said, "Oh, my God!"

Teresa and Elizabeth were pale as sheets.

"We have to move," he said.

Catherine stared at him. "We have to bury them."

"No," he said. "We must move."

Catherine looked shocked. "But the buzzards! We can't leave them like that."

He looked away. Every minute was crucial.

"I couldn't leave them like that, I couldn't." Her voice was pleading. "Please."

He took a deep breath and glanced at the sun; at least three hours before dark. He thought carefully, then reached behind him, pulled the shovel from his saddlebag, and threw it to the ground.

"Bury them. I must go ahead. After you bury them, keep coming down the trail. Just keep coming. I'll pick you up before dark."

"You're going to leave us." She looked hard at him.

Their eyes locked. "Yes. There's something I must do."

Her tongue moistened her lips, then her face hardened. "Then do what you must," she said, her voice firm.

He wheeled the pinto and cantered south on the trail.

8

After their rampage, the Sioux had raced toward the mountain pass, and in imagination he could hear their whoops of victory. A sinking sun gave him only two hours of light, light needed for tracking. He rode hard, aware that out here the night came down suddenly. Still, he could count on a quarter-moon, which would suit his purposes.

When he finally stopped, the sun was a big red ball perched on the edge of the horizon. He had picked a cover of trees where he would wait till dark, then make his move. The Sioux had gone into the pass, and he too would have to go into it, silently, on foot.

To get the edge, he needed a clue to their campsite. They were four, now armed with rifles, and they were Sioux with the craft of the Indian and the skill of killing. He judged them young, strong, wild, and violent. And they had the odds—all he might have was the element of timing and surprise.

He studied the formation of the rocks, waiting for some clue, and after long scrutiny, his patience was rewarded by the quick flight of three crows, startled by the movement of man.

He estimated they were about twenty yards into the interior, in a flat nook, probably, surrounded by the security of stone. They would be relaxed; they did not expect pursuit—cavalry did not protect small wagon units. And they might be hungover from the booze they had grabbed from the wagons. Still, they had the odds.

His shrewdest move would have been to avoid them, but that risk was too great. Eventually they would have sniffed him out, then picked the time and place for attack.

This was his best solution. He'd stay here after dark, move like a ghost; to step on a dry twig would be fatal.

He felt uneasy thinking of the women back with the wagon. Sitting alone out there, they were lambs for slaughter, and they couldn't be feeling good, burying mangled bodies. It would be roughly three hours, he had said, before he could rejoin them—ridiculous, he now realized, for it might be deep into the night before he could even make his first move against the Sioux. He imagined Catherine's thoughts if he didn't turn up after the expected time. But to make a move too soon would be fatal. Tough—they'd just have to sweat it. He thought suddenly of Teresa, that silky body, and what a great way to kill time if he had her there for fun and games.

He checked his guns, gave the pinto its oats, chewed jerky beef, and waited. Patience was a survival trait; you had to act when the time was right.

The night hit fast, and he looked at the great stars flung across the sky in a crazy pattern, except for the Big Dipper. The north star glowed brighter than the others, and the quarter-moon climbing up cast a dim light on the earth. He let himself sleep for a time, then woke, as if from a signal in the depth of his mind.

He felt strong, clear-minded, ready.

He listened carefully. Only the sound of night animals, a coyote skulking in the bushes, a flutter of wings, the hum of insects. He stretched his muscles, then began to move, a few feet at a time, using every cover he could find. He never put his foot down until it was clear what would be stepped on.

In this way, he reached the side of the mountain and worked a slow, circuitous route in, toward the nook where he had pinpointed the Sioux campsite. The knife was in his hand, for silent killing.

He crept between rocks, moved, stopped, listened: only the sound of a coyote baying at the moon, the trickle of water hidden between rocks. He moved, step by step, on flat ground. Under the dim light of the moon he saw prints of moccasins on the path curving sharply behind a cover of rocks.

He leaned forward, knife in his right hand, listened; he

felt that if he listened hard enough he'd hear their breathing.

Then he heard the soft crunch; it was behind him, and every nerve in his body screamed. He wheeled, and there was the Sioux, his face hideous with streaks of red war paint, his eyes fiercely glaring, his teeth clenched and his tomahawk raised for the kill.

Fargo's movements were never thought out—thought could never be that fast; it was all instinct. His powerful arm went up, stopped the downward thrust of the arm with the tomahawk; his other arm struck at the throat with his knife, slashing the windpipe and voice box, then a cradle movement to lower the nerveless body as it started its throes of dying. Blood from the Indian's throat gushed over his arm, and the smell of his sweat was strong in his nostrils. For one moment he looked into the eyes of the Indian, who looked at him as he died, the light of his life starting to go glassy.

Then from behind the rocks he heard a grunt, then a movement. It was impossible to keep sound from an Indian even while he slept. One of them surely had stirred, aware of something. Should he rush in shooting? No there were three of them, and they had guns.

Perhaps the others were already awake. Where had this dead one come from? He knew one thing—a Sioux had moved and spoken and might come out to look. Still, they could not be expecting a single intruder, not in their own camp, not here and now. He counted on this lack of alertness, as he waited, frozen. Any move would betray him.

So he waited, knife in his right hand, gun in his left.

Another grunt, a bit less sleepy.

It was a question; an answer was expected.

Then silence.

Deep, threatening silence. He strained his ears. Nothing. He could hear nothing, but something deep in him smelled danger, and he brought his knife back. The shadow of rock lay over him, and it could be an edge. Then, without a sound, the Sioux appeared at the corner, rifle at the ready looking for his target, but already the knife was hurtling through space. It hit the heart with a thump. Though his body was jolted, the Sioux managed

76

to pull the trigger, and the bullet splintered the rock behind Fargo.

The Sioux was grabbing at his chest, not yet dead, but Fargo was scrambling to get past him, blocked for precious seconds by the body, so that by the time he rounded the corner the other two had already scrambled for cover behind rocks. Two inches of a Sioux's head was still visible, and Fargo's gun, as if with an instinct of its own, spat fire, shearing off part of the skull. He heard the thump of the body as it fell. He moved cautiously to the rock edge and peered out, and a bullet whistled a quarter inch from his ear. He pulled back in a crouch, every nerve in a strain to catch the smallest sound, his eyes racing over the surrounding stone, gauging if it could be used for defense or offense. His mind worked with lightning speed, focusing on what he would do if he were behind that rock and was conditioned, like a Sioux, to act offensively. The rocks were perched on each other, facing him like a wall, going up twenty feet, where there was an opening from which a man could look through and pour down firepower. The other line of attack would be frontal, and the Sioux wouldn't try it, especially with someone able to dispose of his three comrades.

Climbing the twenty feet of rock would be easy for a young Sioux brave, and he'd do it without a sound. It would take only minutes for him to figure out that strategy; in fact, Fargo thought, he might already be on his way up. A small boulder two steps to his right gave cover, and he was behind it in seconds, his eyes glued to the opening over his head.

But nothing happened, neither sound nor sight. He waited, muscles tense, his eyes fixed on the opening. Nothing. Eventually his gaze went down to the brave who had fallen behind the rock. From his position he could see the upper part of his torso; part of his skull was blown away, and his eyes were staring sightlessly at the sky. Like most Sioux, he had a well-muscled body, and he couldn't be more than twenty-one. He looked peaceful enough, and you'd never think that only yesterday he had scalped and raped like a madman. Death brings peace to violent men, he thought, and then he heard the whisper of a sound from behind him, and even before he pieced it together he had wheeled and fired at the sound, and his bullet tore into the red face of the brave who had somehow managed to climb an impossible buildup of rocks to get behind him. The Sioux hadn't had time to bring up his rifle, and the shot had flung him back, his body tumbling and hitting the stone bottom with a sickening thud.

Fargo moved with soft step around the column of rock. The Sioux lay sprawled on his face, arms spread wide; even if the bullet hadn't killed him he'd have been broken by the fall.

Fargo gritted his teeth. He'd been woolgathering and had been saved only by his lightning reflexes, triggered by the scratch of a sound made by breech clout touching stone. He couldn't afford to be that careless, not again; you didn't get a second chance.

He started for his campsite, glancing briefly at the bodies. Well, he had done the job, finished off this gang of killing hyenas. He had avenged those dead women, taken in violence. And he had reopened the trail to Aberdeen, at least for now.

The pinto at sight of him perked its ears and threw its head. He stroked the silky nose and felt the pleasure of kinship with this friend, ally, companion.

It was still deep in the night; he would grab a couple of hours of sleep and start back at the crack of dawn.

He lay down, suddenly aware of how tired he felt. Still, he could take satisfaction. He had cleared away the Sioux.

As he drifted into the maze of sleep, the thought formed in his mind: But there would be more, more Sioux. . . .

9

When he woke early, the sky was still dirty gray, and in
his hurry to join up with the wagon, he did not stop for
breakfast, just dashed a bit of water from his canteen over
his face. He saddled the pinto, pushed it hard, and as he
rode the gray drained out of the sky, the vegetation
turned bright green, and the terrain took on the smiling
face of summer.

A deceptive country, he thought, smiling with inno-
cence one moment and bloody with death the next. It was
why he felt nagging concern for the women alone on the
trail in a wagon. It was pointless to worry now; he had
made the decision already that it was the best choice of
two evils, and if they were still all right, then he would
have done the right thing.

After another hour of riding, he began to feel uneasy,
aware that if they had listened to him, he could have
picked them up by this time. Just ahead was a split in the
trail, a side road, and it was there he found the wagon
tracks. Clearly they had turned in here and pitched a
campsite nearby. And that, in fact, was where he found
the wagon, all of them inside, sleeping in spite of the sun
a quarter up in the sky.

His approach to the wagon, to his disgust, had gone
unchallenged in spite of his being as noisy as possible. He
looked inside, and there they were, snoring up a storm;
they had survived with the dumb luck of innocents.

He pounded the side of the wagon. "Get up, get up,
time for breakfast."

He watched as they came slowly to life, rubbing the
sleep from their eyes. They wore pantalettes, which
curved tightly around their womanly hips, and the upper
part of their breasts were plain to see.

Then they snapped awake and smiled happily at sight of him, even Catherine.

"Oh, my God, it's good to see you!" Teresa gushed.

"Oh yes, yes," Elizabeth said, her dark eyes glittering with excitement.

But Catherine, always a woman with self-control, said, "Yes, Mr. Fargo, it's good to see you, but please, you must give us our privacy for a few minutes."

"Let's rustle up breakfast," he growled.

It was Elizabeth who made it out first, tossing a glad eye at him as she got the coffee pot on the boil and the bacon frying.

Teresa and Catherine came out finally, looking morning-fresh, and it gave him a shot of pleasure looking at their pink, scrubbed faces. After his hard siege with the Sioux, it was pure pleasure to look again at pretty women.

Elizabeth put out his coffee and bacon, then in a shocked voice asked, "Are you wounded?"

The other women turned sharply.

"No, why?"

"Your arm—it's all bloody."

He scowled. It was bloody, the dried blood of the Sioux whose throat he had cut. Preoccupied by other things, he hadn't noticed it.

"Oh," he said casually, "it's not my wound." He poured water from his canteen and rubbed at the arm but some stain of the red was still left. He'd have to wait until they reached a creek where he could soap and soak.

"How'd it happen, Mr. Fargo?" asked Catherine, picking up her coffee.

"What?"

She pointed to his arm. "Not your blood? Indian, I suppose."

He looked at her.

"How many were there, Mr. Fargo?" asked Elizabeth.

He smiled, just drank his coffee. The women looked at Catherine.

"We're not exactly dumb, Mr. Fargo. We knew what you were trying to do." Catherine's blue eyes were studying him.

"What was that?"

"Oh, we discussed it," she said. "That was a brutal

massacre. It was horrible to bury those people. It's something we shall never forget. And I must say it left us bloodthirsty for revenge—all of us."

"We hoped," said Elizabeth, "that you would punish them."

They all looked at him and waited.

"Did you, Mr. Fargo? Did you punish them?" she demanded. "You look as if you had an encounter."

"I don't think they'll give trouble anymore—not to anyone," he said gruffly.

The women smiled at each other.

Elizabeth looked at him admiringly. "I can't tell you how much it means to have you with us. We all agree, this country looks like heaven, but it can be turned into hell quick enough."

He nodded. "That's the way it is here in the territory. And you're never to forget it. If I'm forced to leave you again during this trip, which I hope to avoid, you must post a guard. If I had been a crazy Indian and found your wagon, and you all sleeping, just think of the fun."

They looked at him, their faces serious.

Then Catherine spoke, her face stern. "I hope you're not planning to leave us again, Mr. Fargo. I don't think I can permit that."

He stared at her. "Permit it, Miss Catherine?"

"I think I have to remind you that I am paying you an extremely generous fee to get us to Aberdeen. I am your employer in this case, and have the right to demand certain conditions."

There she was again, with that stiff poker up her ass. Not even a massacre could melt her down.

His smile was thin. "Miss Catherine, I will do what I have to do, where, when, and how I decide to do it."

Her eyes were sparks of fire. He headed her off. "But I'm not after throwing three beauties to the wolves. So relax, and get the wagon rolling."

The wagon rumbled along, and he, as usual, rode in front or behind it, his senses alert. The land went monotonously flat for a time, which gave him a long view, and the peace of the landscape eased his tension. He felt it would be a quiet day, but kept a sharp eye on the clues of the trail.

The land began to slope up, grow hilly, thicken with bush growths and trees, and when the sun was riding high they hit a broad stream.

They pitched camp, and he brought the pinto to the sparkling water, let it drink, filled the canteens. Then he went up a piece, behind some bushes, peeled his clothes, and swam and kicked about in the fresh water. It was a good feeling to be clean of sweat. Downstream, he could hear the women's voices, screeching a bit as they romped, just as glad as he to wipe the sweat of travel off their bodies.

It didn't take much imagination to picture them frolicking about. Nothing, he thought, would be nicer than to throw a pitch at Teresa later. The thought of her voluptuous body started a bit of lust up. He could, of course, invite her to a party. It's a free country, he thought, and though Catherine might be sour on the idea, she couldn't stop it.

He put a nosebag with oats on the pinto, then sat down to a lunch of beans, peas, collards. Not too appetizing, he thought.

The rising slope of ground during the afternoon made it a hard pull; it slowed their headway, forcing them to stop twice to rest the horses.

That afternoon, riding easy on the trail, his eye restlessly scanned the mountainside and he felt a tingle of tension. The contour of stone wasn't quite right. A shape seemed to blend into the stone background, yet oddly, it looked human. The jogging of the pinto marred his concentration, so he reined up and stared; the contour solidified, moved slightly, and then he became aware of a familiar figure; it was not only a Sioux, but a special one: Red Sun.

He raised his hand in a slow wave.

There was no answer, no recognition. A slight move and the figure was gone into the recesses of the rocks.

He frowned, then put the pinto into a trot. When he caught up to the wagon, Catherine threw him a questioning look.

"Something worrying you, Mr. Fargo?"

He gave a slow grin. "Not much worries me."

But the incident nibbled at his mind. It might not have been Red Sun after all, just a Sioux with his build. But he felt inclined to trust his judgment that it was Red Sun, and that being so, why was he following them, or, more to the point, why hadn't he responded to the wave of friendship?

It was hostile, no two ways about it, as if you had put out your hand, and the other man had turned his back on you.

What did it mean?

That rider, he realized, was on the mountainside, and good scouting would turn up four Sioux dead by knife and gun. Scouting also would turn up his prints, very familiar to Red Sun.

So Red Sun knew that he had committed mayhem among the braves of his tribe. But the braves had done their share of slaughter. Surely he would understand. Yes, he'd understand.

But perhaps for Red Sun, blood was thicker than understanding. If Red Sun were to become hostile, that would turn up one hell of a problem.

He had never, in all his experience on the trail, met up with a white or red man who challenged his inner belief that, in a man-to-man confrontation, he would come out on top. But he did not have that feeling with Red Sun. He sensed great reserves of power in this Sioux. Red Sun had trailsmanship, endurance, and intelligence, and a great talent for survival. He smiled; Red Sun, in a way, was his redskin counterpart. He grinned at his thought: What the hell, I'd hate to slug it out with someone like me.

Then he became aware that he had been tracking a deer, almost mechanically. The thought hit him that venison steaks would be a nice change of diet.

The tracks were fresh, and if he acted quickly he wouldn't lose too much time. He pressed on past trees, scrub bushes, thickets, then stopped and whistled. He studied the ground: big claw tracks, also fresh, of a mountain lion had started to trail the deer. He pressed on faster and, to his relief, noticed the lion tracks veer west abruptly; perhaps it had sniffed closer and easier game.

He caught up with the deer in a heavy thicket, a young

buck that stopped with fatal curiosity to stare at him. In sudden alarm it started to scamper, but a shot to the heart from his rifle brought it down. He skinned the deer and quartered the meat, put it into leather pouches, tied them to his saddle, then cantered back. He reached the wagon just before dusk, and they camped near a clump of oaks.

"Fresh deer meat for dinner," he said with a grin. They watched as he unpacked the red meat from his saddle.

Catherine gave him a hard eye. "Do we have to kill such beautiful animals?" she demanded.

He glowered at her. "Just in case you don't yet know it, Miss Catherine, man has to kill to eat."

She shrugged. "I won't argue with you. It's possible for us to live on vegetables and fruits."

"If you call that living," he grumbled. "And on the trail, we eat anything we can grab. And be grateful." He grinned. "I don't think you'll turn away from the smell of fried venison."

"I, for one, won't eat it," she said firmly.

"Mr. Fargo needs red meat," said Teresa. "Isn't that what makes him a red-blooded man?"

Catherine threw her a withering look, but Fargo just grinned and winked at Teresa. Her breasts strained against her gray garment, and he thought of their last encounter. He felt red-blooded right now, and wouldn't mind a rough-and-tumble with her. He wondered if she had caught his wink.

Then he heard the pinto—the neighing with an agonized pitch that could mean just one thing.

"Don't move," he hissed, his gun out with lightning speed, sliding forward in a crouch toward the horse tied about 150 feet away.

Then he saw the slinking silhouette, the mountain lion, its muscular body starting a run at the pinto. It made a great lunge and was still in the air when his gun barked twice; suddenly all the terrible force of that powerful body went out, like an exploded bag, and it dropped to the earth, dead weight, its legs twisting only for a moment.

It happened with such great speed that the women, though bug-eyed with excitement, didn't have time to experience fear.

He walked to the lion and looked at it: a young female with a sleek, bullet body, cruel claws, looking in death more like a giant brown pussycat. He had hit the right eye with both shots to get its brain, and dark blood oozed from the sightless wound. A neat bit of shooting, he thought.

Catherine came up first, hand on her breast. "My God, what made it come here, into the camp?"

"Smell of fresh meat. The deer. Must have been damned hungry to try this."

"It came after the deer?" she asked, her eyes narrowing.

He looked at her, then said, "We'll have to camp down about five hundred yards." He walked to the pinto; its eyes were glaring, its flank still quivering at the closeness of a terrible enemy, even though dead. He kept stroking the pinto to calm it, then walked it off.

Later, at their new camp, he sliced the venison, put the strips into the frypan, and watched them sizzle.

When the steaks were brown, filling the air with delicious aroma, ready to eat, Catherine threw a yearning glance at them, but, being a hardhead, he thought, she stuck to her decision and ate her kale and collards. He, on the other hand, found his big cut of steak tasty, tender, juicy. Teresa and Elizabeth too seemed to be enjoying the steaks. The sight of Catherine scooping up her limp food amused him, and he couldn't resist the needle. "Looks like a great dinner of stewed weeds and grass you've got there, Miss Catherine."

She threw him a hard look. "At least I'm not disturbed by the thought that a beautiful animal has been destroyed to make food for me."

He cut a small piece of steak, looked at it with pleasure. "Ain't nothing disturbing my taste of a great hunk of meat."

"In your case, not much would," she said grimly.

Teresa and Elizabeth looked at each other and smiled. Catherine scowled at them and went into a deep silence. She's gonna hit me in the balls in a minute, he thought, chewing on a slice.

Then she caught his eye. "You say, Mr. Fargo, that the

lion broke into our camp because of the smell of fresh meat. That would be the deer that you killed?"

"That's the story."

"Then you had to kill the lion?"

"Yup."

"You know, Mr. Fargo, you are an excellent guide, we all agree, but I think you have to admit you surround us with death and destruction. Within the space of an hour, a dead deer and a dead lion."

He smiled genially. "It goes with the territory, miss."

"Well," she said, "it'd be nice if we could travel without always having to worry about when death and destruction will strike next."

His mouth twisted with amusement. "That would be nice. But I wouldn't count on it."

"It seems to me," said Elizabeth, "that Mr. Fargo has been keeping us *from* death and destruction, Catherine."

Catherine glared at her. "I think, Elizabeth, that your judgment is a bit clouded by the fact that Mr. Fargo is the only man around."

Fargo laughed. He wished to hell *she* would act as if he were the only man around. Catherine was a beautiful woman, built with more curves than a country road, but she was surrounded by armor; she might as well be a nun.

When later that night he lay in his bedroll, on a hill curved away from the wagon where they slept, his mind drifted back to Red Sun, and he worried again why the Sioux had not returned his salute. There could be small doubt that a master tracker like Red Sun had already discovered his attack on the rampaging Sioux. It was wise to believe that he had found these comrades of his all shot up, and it had angered him. He might be thinking of revenge. If that was so, there wouldn't be one easy moment left in the mileage to Aberdeen. Red Sun, however, had a nobility about him, and if he had decided on revenge, he'd not attack without a declaration of war. Yes, Fargo thought, at least he could expect that, so he could relax for now. The thought of Clay flashed through his mind, with the invariable sting of anger. But there was small point thinking about Clay when there was, at the moment, no guarantee he'd get to Aberdeen. The killing of the four

Sioux must in time bring on, as a point of honor, an attack by other braves.

For now, however, the terrain looked peaceful enough, and he could ease up and get a night's sleep.

The stars were pieces of silver in the night sky, and he looked at them as always before sleeping. Then he turned restlessly, suddenly aware of the hunger of his body for a woman.

Then he smiled: He had picked up a sound, light, secretive, but not a threatening sound, one he figured made by Teresa on her way to his bedroll. Curious, he thought, how the body would reveal its hunger when it discovered someone close by to satisfy that hunger.

She came up the hill around the tree to his bedroll, and it was Elizabeth!

She was wearing her pantalettes, which clung to a voluptuous body that, all day, was concealed by her sexless nun garment.

He stared at her face, smiling at him. Elizabeth! How in hell had that happened? Not that he was, for one moment, ungrateful. He did have a zestful taste for women in their many varieties, and Elizabeth was one sweet specimen of her sex.

"Elizabeth. I'm glad to discover that you walk in your sleep."

She smiled. "Well, the fact is, I couldn't sleep, thinking of how mean Catherine was to you."

"You think she was mean?" She looked a tempting piece with her pantalettes tight against her hips, which curved into a slender waist. She had nicely formed breasts, and he could see her cleavage. She was a brunette with white skin, an oval face, dark glittering eyes, and a ready warm smile. From the beginning he was caught by her warmth and femininity, her quickness to laugh.

"Oh, yes, she was mean," Elizabeth said, "but Catherine is good-hearted. She can be a bit stern, but I suppose it's because she's been put in charge of us, feels responsible."

"Yes, she's one starchy lady," he said.

"How long before we get to Aberdeen?" she asked, sitting down, hunched with her arms around her knees.

He was surprised at her casual air, especially as he was

lying bare-chested, and in his shorts. Although she seemed casual, her gaze kept returning, compulsively, to the large bunch-up in his crotch.

"That depends," he said. "I take it one mile at a time."

Her face became serious. "Do you expect more trouble?"

"It's best to expect it, but hope it doesn't happen."

She put her arms back, and her breasts were thrust out. "I haven't been sleeping well. I keep thinking about those poor women. Such a terrible end."

He said nothing. It couldn't be easy for a woman to wipe out such a sight.

Her lip trembled. "The other night I dreamed we were attacked by Indians. Woke up in a terrible sweat."

He smiled. "It'll be all right, Elizabeth."

She smiled back bravely. "In the dream an Indian had me down, was strangling me. I tried to scream. Thought I was finished. Then I heard a shot and he fell off my body—dead. You had saved me."

He grinned. "A good dream." He had saved Teresa and Catherine from that fate worse than death, he thought. Perhaps Elizabeth felt left out, and had her experience of it in a dream. That would be strange.

She laughed. "The dream left me feeling very grateful to you. I wanted to do something to show my appreciation."

He laughed. She was hungry, just as he was, and she had gone through a nice little act to get to this point.

"C'mere," he said, holding out his hands.

She looked at him, eyes glowing, then she stood and walked over. She stood there above him, and he rose to his knees and pulled at the bodice, so that her breasts swiftly spilled out. They were nice and full, beautifully shaped, with soft pink nipples. He put his hands over them, they were silky to his touch. He put his lips to one, nuzzled it, caressed the other. He felt the nipples harden; he flicked his tongue over one and then rose to his feet and kissed her mouth. She flung her arms around him, held him tightly, as if he might get away.

He kissed her again, a sweet-tasting mouth, then he dropped and pulled down her pantalettes. She stepped out of them, and nude, she was delicious-looking, with fine curving hips, flat belly, molded thighs and legs, and a tangled dark bush.

He let his finger caress the edge of the opening, finally pressing through to the lush warmth within. A deep sigh came from her lips; she seemed to be in a trance. He continued to stroke, and as he went on and on her body went suddenly taut and she grabbed him, her teeth clenched. "Oh," she breathed. He waited a moment, then slipped off his shorts. She looked down at his fierce excitement, dropped to her knees, and pressed her cheek against his large, aroused organ. The skin of her face was like velvet, but her lips were still softer, and she kissed him, and then her lips opened, and he felt the depths of her marvelous mouth. Her thirst for love seemed unquenchable, and waves of pleasure went over him until finally he withdrew from her, let his hands go gently over the pillowed firm buttocks, his palms pleasuring in their contours. Then gently he lowered her onto his bedroll, where she widened her legs, and he entered her slowly, piercing the velvet softness, she waiting until he penetrated completely. Again a deep sigh.

He put his hands behind her buttocks and began to move, a rhythm that stayed slow, steady, and relentless. Every so often her body would coil and tighten as though she were experiencing some intolerable agony; he went on and on, the pleasure rising. Then she began to breathe his name over and over, her arms tight around him, her body arching now to receive the rhythm of his thrusts. On and on he thrust relentlessly, while she went into some private controlled frenzy until he felt the excruciating pleasure, felt the great swelling, felt her totally engulf him. A stifled scream escaped her lips, then silence, just the tremor of her body. They stayed together, locked in an unbreakable embrace, until the passion drained, and her body went still.

Then finally he came away. He looked at her silky white body next to him, the slender waist, the rising breasts, the fine sweep of hip. A great piece of woman, he thought.

Her eyes were on him. "Fargo, Fargo," she said, and grabbed his face, kissed him.

Afterward, when she had gone, he slipped on his

shorts. The stars were still up there, glittering in the night, but he felt a deep calm; the tension of his body was all gone.

He settled in the bedroll.

Tomorrow ought to be a good day, he thought.

Then he thought of Red Sun. . . .

10

The day, however, started off far from beautiful; in fact, the southeast sky was heavy with a bloat of clouds. A bit later they were hit by a light flurry of rain. Then a vigorous west wind sent the clouds scurrying east, and within the hour the sky shone radiantly blue.

Because of the clarity of the air, he could see the sculptured detail of the mountain, the grandeur of its peaks and crags.

He stayed on edge, aware that by now the Sioux must have discovered that massacre could be a two-way game. And they would come, bent on revenge; a war party in force.

That afternoon, as he cantered ahead of the wagon, he picked up a movement so slight that he might have put it off if he had not been so nerved up. The movement seemed to stop when he did, which he contrived deliberately.

It was a master tracker, and his instinct told him it was Red Sun.

It's not enemy action, he thought. No, just now it was surveillance, but later it could be hostile.

At the Black Rock crossing, a trail going from east to west, he picked up the fresh tracks of a four-wagon train. He spent a few minutes looking at them and thinking. Four wagons meant firepower, and he needed all the firepower he could find, and that in a damned hurry. They needed his guns too, for that matter. The territory was hot just now: the white man and red man were caught in a cycle of revenge, and survival came only to the stronger. It was smart to expect a Sioux war party would pick up this wagon train just as it would pick him up. The best defensive tactic was for the wagons to join together.

He raced the pinto back to the wagon and signaled a stop for lunch to Catherine. When they got to the coffee, he put it to them casually.

"We're gonna have company," he said.

They looked quizzical. "Such as?" asked Catherine.

"There's a four-wagon train up ahead of us. We're going to join them."

"Four wagons, Mr. Fargo? Wouldn't that slow us down?"

"It might slow us down, but it'd build up our strength. Five men are stronger than one."

"Expecting an attack, Mr. Fargo?"

"Yes, I am."

"Why?"

"We've got to expect that a war party of Sioux will be scouting the terrain. They must know about the wagons ahead. We're caught in the action."

"What if we strike out on our own? Perhaps the Sioux won't bother us."

He smiled. "They'd bother us. It's good war tactics to pick off the weak enemy first. And the braves have a taste for the white squaw."

Catherine's blue eyes glittered. "How do you know there's a war party? Have you seen something?"

He smiled grimly. "I smell them." Why tell her that even if the Sioux were not after that wagon train, something hard to believe, still a war party of revenge would come, because of the Sioux he had destroyed? They had a code of revenge.

"If Mr. Fargo thinks it's the right thing to do," said Elizabeth, "we should do it."

"I agree," said Teresa.

"Mr. Fargo is very competent with a gun. I don't deny that for a moment. It's his judgment that I question."

He rubbed his chin, then said, "I'm afraid we have no choice. The Sioux will be coming out of the rocks. One man and three women won't be able to stop them."

"Are you sure of that? That we have no choice? Why don't we have any choice?"

He grimaced. "I've explained it."

"Is it because you destroyed the four Indians, perhaps?"

The shrewd bitch, she could read him.

"That might have something to do with it," he admitted. "But it had to be done. They stood in our way. They could have played that bloody game with us."

"They could, they could . . . but we don't know that *for sure*. Now that you have done your damage, there's no doubt about a war party for revenge, is there? In other words, Mr. Fargo, you have turned a possible attack into a sure one."

He stared: she had the gift of proving black was white, a bitch, a birdbrain, but dammit, she did have a sliver of reason in her argument. How in hell could he answer her? Could any answer convince her?

"Listen, in my judgment that massacre gang of Sioux would try the same thing on us. *My* judgment. And that's how we move on this trail, lady!"

She scowled at him but said nothing.

"But we have no choice, now, Catherine," said Elizabeth.

"No, it seems we have none—now," Catherine said.

There was silence.

"It's agreed, then—we join the wagon train?" he asked.

He wanted their consent, because later, when they found themselves in the midst of death and destruction, they would at least feel part of the decision.

The women nodded.

He put down his coffee cup. "If we pick up our pace just a bit, we'll reach that wagon train in the late afternoon."

They made good time on the trail; he moved out ahead and a quick canter brought him in sight of the four-wagon train. He decided to approach them from the west, so they'd have a good look at him; strangers made settlers nervous, and they liked to see where your hands were. These men driving the wagons were from the East, and it could give them small comfort to see a stranger holstering two guns.

They were four wagons moving south at a measured pace, three driven by a man with a woman alongside. The lead driver in a red-checked shirt was alone.

Fargo signaled him, and he pulled his horses to a stop.

He had a hard face and narrow eyes, and he squinted suspiciously, picked up his rifle.

"The name is Fargo," he said.

"I suppose that's important to know," the driver said.

The accent was Eastern, maybe Ohio, a farmer out to make a grab for a rich piece of land in the West. Fargo watched the way the man held the rifle: this muttonhead could shoot before he understood anything.

"I've got a wagon with three women coming up behind you. We're headed for Aberdeen. It's on this trail."

The man looked at Fargo, his size, his clothes, his guns.

"So what about it?"

Fargo smiled. A real dude, he did not volunteer his name, which was custom in the West, and he was rude. But he was a dude, and it was best to make allowance.

"Well, you seem to going our way. We'd be happy to join you."

The man scowled. "Why?"

He smiled. "It's a good idea to bunch up with other wagons when you're on the trail. Good for company. Good for defense."

The scowl still there. "We're not moving fast. One of our horses is just getting over a lame leg. You'd be better off pushing on by yourself."

Two other riders, by this time, came walking up, also carrying rifles. They looked him over.

"What's the trouble, Madden?" asked one, nodding to Fargo. He was square-jawed, blue-eyed; the other was bearded, brown-eyed, with a round black hat. Fargo smiled genially, introduced himself.

"Skye Fargo's the name."

Square jaw nodded. "I'm Jones, this is Clark. What's it about, Madden?"

"This feller says he has a wagon with three women going to Aberdeen, wants to join our train."

"What's wrong with that?"

"Well, we've got a slow train here," Madden said, scowling.

"That's right," said Jones. "We're moving slow. Why join us?"

"He thinks we'd make good company," Madden said sarcastically.

Fargo smiled grimly. "You know, this is Sioux country."

"Yeah, we know," Madden said.

"They've been wild."

They stared at him.

"How do you know?" Madden asked.

"A massacre. We passed two wagons that were hit."

That jarred them; at least it did Jones and Clark, who went grim-faced, but Madden's eyes narrowed with suspicion. "When was that?"

"Two days ago."

"And you passed through, just one man. How'd you get through?"

The men looked at him.

"I took hostile action," he said.

"What's that mean?" demanded Madden.

"Yeah," Jones chimed in. "What do you mean, 'hostile action'?"

"There were four raiders. I tracked them to their hideout. Caught them by surprise."

There was a long silence.

Then Madden's voice, heavy with disbelief. "You telling us, mister, that you tracked four Sioux and killed them, all of them?"

Fargo smiled slow. "It sounds like that, doesn't it?"

Another man, the last driver, had come up, a lean, clean-shaven man with a hard jaw and blue eyes, and he too carried a rifle. He had heard the last interchange.

"This is Skye Fargo," said Madden. "Did you hear what he just said, Smitty?" His attitude to Smitty, Fargo noted, was polite.

Smitty's hard blue eyes looked at his guns and his build. "I've heard of Fargo." His smile was friendly. "Best trailsman in the territory. If he says he's knocked out four Sioux, I'd believe him."

The men turned to look again at him, with more respect.

Then Jones spoke. "I'm sorry if we're not friendly. We worry about strangers." He turned to Smitty. "He says there could be a war party nearby, and he wants to join us."

"I'd be much obliged if a man like Fargo wants to join us," said Smitty. He looked at Fargo. "What makes you think there's a war party nearby?"

"I think it's smart to believe that."

Madden was looking embarrassed. "I'm sorry, Fargo. I've heard wild stories about trail bums who trick their way into your train and then do their dirty work. If I talked hard, I'm sorry. You're welcome to join us."

"That's right, partner," said Jones.

Clark smiled.

He grinned at them. "Much obliged, gents."

Within the half hour, he brought the women and their wagon up and took the last position in the train.

Fargo rode point for the wagon train, scanning the landscape, scrutinizing possible ambush sites, paying particular mind to the side of the mountain. Nothing, no scurry of birds, no scamper of animals, just a hard sun beating down heat.

Madden had told the truth about the wagon train; it dragged its ass like a crippled steer. That not only lost them time, but could set them up for trouble. The Sioux were out there even if not visible; it was better to believe that, he told the men, because preparation was half the battle.

When they stopped to eat, the wives and youngsters came out; the women, matronly, well fleshed, bonneted, bustled about their men and kids. Because water and food were crucial, it had been arranged that each family be responsible for itself, but still there was sharing.

When the women of his wagon came out in their nuns' habits, it jarred the settlers for the moment, and it amused Fargo to see the deference paid the ladies as members of the church. But soon everything became routine; the settlers were preoccupied with the challenge of making do in an alien environment.

During the meal, Fargo listened to the wives clucking over the eating habits of the children, moaning about the lack of soap and water, the abundance of dirt, the deadly diet of beans, the heat of the sun; they yearned for a homestead.

Fargo, watching the kids romp, the mothers cluck, felt a mix of emotions. They had come out to the territory, endured a world of hardship with the hope of a better life, but they might have to run a gauntlet of fire to reach it. The Sioux were not about to give up without a struggle the land they loved, the land of their ancestors, not to a pack of palefaces from the East.

He felt a sting of anger at these men who seemed willing to expose their families to bloodshed for a piece of land. Men like Madden were in a hurry to get out there first, for the best pickings; they wouldn't wait to travel with the big wagon trains, which sometimes had armed escort.

The memory of the massacre was still fresh in his mind, and thinking of it made him grit his teeth.

Tomorrow, before dawn, he'd get up and take care of something that had been nibbling at his mind.

Hours later, the blanket of night lay over the campsite, the wagons were quiet. He was lying on his back in a nook surrounded by trees, a site he had picked for his bedroll, when, to his surprise, he saw Teresa approach. Jones, who was on guard duty, surely must have seen her, and Fargo leaned on an elbow, frowned, and watched her. She wore that long gray garment, and it was hard for him not to think of her as a nun. The last time she had come to him, she had worn pantalettes; her long red hair had curled to her shoulders, and her marvelous breasts and his own horniness had put them into a blistering embrace. But now she wore that garment of purity, and Jones, if he was any kind of a lookout, must have seen her moving in his direction. If he let her stay for any length of time, it might give Jones a quaint idea of the nuns in his wagon.

"Isn't it late for you, Teresa? You should be in the wagon."

Her eyes were glittering. "It's never too late for you, Fargo."

He had to grin. She looked as horny as a toad, but he wasn't buying.

"It's not a good time, Teresa."

She looked reproachful. "You made time for Elizabeth the other night."

The statement startled him.

"Oh, yes, I know about it," she said.

He shrugged. "Well, it's different now. We may be sitting on dynamite."

"The Sioux?"

He nodded.

"It's frightening," she said, sitting next to him. "I'm thinking of the women we buried."

He just looked at her. What could he say?

"Such a thing could happen here, couldn't it?" she asked.

He smiled. "We have at least five rifles. That's firepower."

She moved closer. "I'm glad you're with us. It makes me feel safer."

He watched as she pushed her cowl back, which let her flaming red hair cascade about her face. Somehow it turned her from a nun into a nymph. He became aware of her breasts, thrusting heavily against the dress, and her eyes, glittering wickedly, her full lips half open with hunger.

"Well, don't feel too safe," he said. He was lying there in his shorts, and in spite of his belief the situation was wrong, his body responded. And something in the primitive instinct of the female, he thought, tells her when that's happening.

Because she slid closer.

But the whole thing was wrong; the wagons only a hundred feet away, Jones aware she was prowling, and that nun's garment, and the pantalettes under that which would take a helluva time to remove. He was horny, but the situation was wrong.

"You must go back, Teresa. There isn't time."

She scowled. She looked frustrated. She looked at the bulge in his shorts, then smiled.

"But you don't want me to go."

He drew a deep breath. "I don't, but there just isn't time."

Her hand went out to his bulge. "But there might be time, just for this." And her hand slid under his shorts to

98

touch him. The silk touch of her hand put a great test on his willpower.

Silently he watched as she pulled down his shorts, exposing his frantic flesh.

Her eyes gleamed as she leaned to it, pressing it to her face, then to her lips, looking into his eyes to read his excitement, then turning to it with a smile, opening her mouth, bringing it into the velvety warmth. Moving her lips over it again, again and again, her eyes closed, as if she were experiencing the same intense pleasure that he was. She moved her lips and tongue, touching each part of him, and he watched as in a trance. She moved with instinctive art, and when at last he felt the great surge, he had to grit his teeth, the focused pleasure was so intense. To his amazement, she too fell back, experiencing her own ecstasies.

They lay there, as if both had been hit by a thunderbolt. Then he collected his wits.

"Where in hell did you learn how to do that?" he demanded.

"It comes naturally," she said.

There was a long moment.

"Well," he said, "unless you'd like to ruin the reputation of nuns . . ."

"Yes, yes." She pushed her red hair under the cowl, and with that one movement, she managed to look again like the character role she was playing.

She rose to her feet. "That was wicked, wasn't it, Fargo?"

"Very wicked, but nice."

She smiled. "Weren't there a lot of wicked nuns in the Middle Ages? And they burned them at the stake?"

"That may happen to you if you don't get the hell back to the wagon. And let Jones see you, for God's sake. He'll think we just had a friendly get-together."

She turned and raised her eyebrows. "Isn't that what we did have?"

11

Next morning, before dawn, he found Madden on guard duty, sitting against the spoke of a wheel smoking a clay pipe. Fargo's appearing at that hour, primed with two pistols, astonished him.

"Mighty early to be up and stirring, Fargo."

"I want to scout a bit on the mountainside before the light breaks."

"Scout? For what? Indians?"

"For one Indian." Fargo was smiling.

Madden gazed at him. "And who would that be, Pocahontas?" He laughed at his own joke.

Fargo grinned slowly. A real mulehead. "No. He's called Red Sun. A warrior chief."

Madden's eyes narrowed. "You know him?"

"Yup, I know him."

Madden sat up straight. "How come you know him?"

"How come I know you?"

"Fargo, you're one strange bird. Not anyone I'd want in my wagon. But if Smitty vouches for you, I guess it's all right."

Fargo gave him a cold grin. "But he could be mistaken, you're thinking."

"That's right, Fargo, it's what I'm thinking."

He laughed. "Lucky I have Smitty to vouch for me." He walked to the pinto, saddled it, then rode up to Madden, who had been watching. "If I were you, Madden, I wouldn't sit so damned still. You could set yourself up as a bull's-eye for an arrow. Keep moving and keep looking."

Madden glared. "Just don't bring any redskins back with you."

A real muttonbrain, Fargo thought. as he turned the pinto toward the mountain.

He made good headway in the predawn light and reached the mountainside as the sun peered over the eastern horizon. It shaped up like a great orange, and he would not be surprised if later the sun hit hard against the rocks. He moved through a gorge and found a narrow trail that climbed upward. He moved the pinto carefully, working toward the oddly shaped crag where yesterday he had noticed the small puzzling movement.

When he reached the spot, he dismounted and examined the ground; it was clear that a branch had been used to foul the tracks. He clambered to a large flat rock that gave a long view of the terrain. It was there that he found a light moccasin toed print, typical of the Indian foot. A crease line under the big toe identified it as Red Sun's.

He glanced at the rocks and crevices nearby, stroked his jaw thoughtfully. Then he turned to his broad view of the terrain. A narrow stream meandered southwest, the ground undulated into valleys and hills, and the trail twisted south. From that height the five wagons looked like miniatures huddled together near a tree clump. Nothing in the area looked suspicious.

Could he have been wrong about a war party? It was his nature to expect attack. Perhaps in this case he was wrong. Perhaps they had not yet discovered his four dead Indians. Perhaps they would reach Aberdeen in one piece.

He shook his head. Perhaps he was feeding himself a bunch of loco weed!

The Sioux had to know. Why in hell would Red Sun be on his trail?

The sun climbed, and he could feel the heat off the rocks. He moved back to the flat ground where the pinto stood, sheltered by rock shadows.

He lay against the rocks, legs sprawled on the ground, fingers laced behind his head. There was nothing to do but wait. There had to be surveillance. Thoughts went idly through his mind. Then he remembered how the quick time had been with Teresa, and he felt a tingle of excitement. The sun kept rising and the heat bounced off the rocks.

Then came the sound, if you could call it that; more the breath of a sound. He kept his hands behind his head, kept still as a statue.

Then, as if he had materialized out of the rocks, Red Sun was there in front of him. He looked hugely rugged, with his broad, powerful chest, slender waist, lithe muscular thighs. There was a rifle in his hand and a wicked knife in his belt. His broad face was calm, his brown eyes piercing.

Not much friendliness here, thought Fargo. He put his hand over his heart.

Red Sun ignored it, "Fargo wants to speak with Red Sun?" he asked.

It's trouble, Fargo thought. He spoke solemnly, looking deeply into the sun-flecked brown eyes of the Sioux. "Fargo travels with the white man's wagons. The white man does not wish to fight. He wants only to go west. Without hurt to the Sioux."

Red Sun's eyes were unflinching. "The white man must go back. To the East." Fargo sensed the anger behind the words.

"These are settlers, looking for land. They wish no harm to the Sioux."

Red Sun's features hardened. "The white man does great harm to the Sioux. He destroys our hunting grounds. He kills the buffalo for games, like small boys. He is like the locust on the land."

It's a no-win setup, Fargo thought, but he had to try.

"There are women and children in the white man's wagons. They have done no hurt to the Sioux."

Red Sun's eyes gleamed. "The Sioux will not hurt them if they go back." He folded his arms, and a fierce look appeared on his face. "The white soldiers kill our squaws. Tear their bodies. Show it with much joke. That is the white man and his ways."

It was true; Fargo had heard brutal stories. "Some evil people are everywhere. But these are good people. They wish to go west."

Red Sun raised one arm and waved it in a long semicircle. "This is the land of the Sioux. A land where he can ride as free as the deer. The Sioux cannot live without his free ways. The white man would steal this freedom."

There was a long moment of silence, then brown eyes softened. "Red Sun has thought of Fargo as his blood brother. There is much honor in Fargo." Then the eyes went cold. "Yet Fargo has killed four braves of my tribe."

So Red Sun had known it, all the time. It was why he trailed the wagon. He was a Sioux and Fargo was white. Could it be that after all the difference was unbridgeable?

He spoke slowly. "These four braves have been dishonorable. They have killed, and done bad things to the white women. They would do the same to the women of my wagon. It is a thing I had to do."

There was another long silence as each looked into the other's eyes.

"Who did the first killing?" asked Red Sun finally. "It was the white man. It is cowardly to accept such killing without revenge. The Sioux is a great warrior. He cannot accept the shame of defeat."

They had come to an impasse.

Then Red Sun put his hand over his heart. "You have given me my life and I have given you your life. We should be blood brothers. But the Great Spirit has made our skins of different color. And put the arrow between us."

Fargo felt a rush of warmth for Red Sun. He was a man, every damned inch of him. Still, the crucial question had to be asked.

"Fargo is proud to know the feelings of Red Sun. But he must ask again: Can our wagons go in safety to the west?"

The Sioux's face did not change; it was granite. "When the moon comes up, Red Sun and his braves will be at war with Fargo and the white men."

For a long moment, his eyes burned out of his stern face, then, just before he turned away, the face softened, and the pain glittered in his eyes. After he left, Fargo felt a stab of feeling.

He stood still as a statue, thinking. They both felt a brotherhoood, but hostile forces had thrown them against each other.

It was a collision of races. The expanding white man rushing west in a hunger for land, resisted by the red man who wanted to live in the way of his fathers.

In this collision, many innocents would die.

Fate had just thrown the dice.

And the wagons were in deadly danger.

With a deep sigh, Fargo walked toward the pinto.

He was about to mount up when he thought of something, and though it was a high risk, he followed Red Sun's tracks. Fifteen minutes later, at an empty campsite in a hidden crevice of the mountain, he found what he wanted. He counted them, fifteen prints, roughly. A Sioux war party of fifteen was a deadly force.

Breakfast was just about finished when he made it back to the wagons. The men came forward to meet him, their faces curious.

Smitty gave him a smile. "What'd you find out there, Fargo?"

"Nothing too good," he said.

"What's that mean?" asked Jones, thrusting out his square jaw.

"Yeah," said Madden. "I told 'em you were going out to look for an Indian warrior. Find him?"

"I found him," he said and looked hard into the pale-brown eyes of Madden.

The men picked up his mood and grew tense.

Then Smitty spoke. "Trying to tell us something, Fargo?"

"I think," Fargo said, "that by tomorrow, we should expect all hell to break loose."

There was a long silence. Then Madden scowled. "What the hell kind of scare language is that?"

"Hold it, Madden," said Smitty. "Tell us, plainly, what you've been trying to do."

"Trying to head off the Sioux."

"How could you reach them?" demanded Madden. "They wouldn't let a white man within a mile of them."

"I once did a favor for a chief warrior. I told him we wanted to move west, peaceably."

"What'd he say?" asked Jones.

"He said, 'You can go east, but not west. If you go west, it will be war when the moon goes up tonight.' "

The men looked at each other.

"How many are there?" asked Smitty.

"I'd expect about fifteen."

Then Clark, the man in the round brown hat, spoke.

"I'm for turning back. We could join a bigger train. More guns. Maybe cavalry protection."

Madden scowled. "Listen, we're out in front. It gives us the best choice. We've blistered our behinds getting this far. I don't figure on going back, after all our sacrifice to get this far."

"What about the women and kids?" said Clark. "We're putting their lives on the line."

Then Jones spoke. "I don't like going back. It cost us a lot to get this far. We've got five riflemen, all good shooters. The Indians maybe won't have guns. We'll mow them down."

Smitty looked at Fargo.

"What's your opinion?"

"If I were in your shoes?"

"Yeah."

"I'd go back."

The men looked at him, grim-faced.

"What if we decide to go on?" asked Smitty.

"I'll go with you," Fargo said.

Smitty looked at each of the men. "How about it?"

"We go on," said Madden.

The other men nodded.

From where he stood, Fargo could see, at least three miles away, the scattered boulders alongside the mountain. Boulders like that, he thought, could make good cover. Also, with the mountain on their flank, they could blunt the usual Indian style of attack, the circle. It was now late afternoon, and according to Red Sun, the moonrise would be the Sioux declaration of war. And since Indians didn't particularly care for night warfare, Fargo felt there would be no action until morning.

He pointed out the site to Smitty and Jones. "We should make campsite there tonight. With the mountain on our flank, the Sioux won't be able to circle us. Use the boulders for cover."

"Do you think they'll hit us tomorrow?" asked Smitty.

"They'll hit us when they think we're at our weakest."

"When will that be?"

"I reckon in the morning, when the sun comes up, when it hits our eyes. They'll come in a wave, yelling their brains out. We should be strung out, each roughly defending his own wagon, and shooting at the Sioux directly in front. The women must shoot too; they might hit something. And, this above all, we should be out there and waiting."

"Will they all have rifles, do you think?" Smitty's face was grim.

"I doubt it. Half of them, I reckon. But they'll have flaming arrows. That can be worse than a bullet. You can't travel in a burned-out wagon."

When the wagon train left the trail and rumbled toward the mountain, it did not, naturally, go unnoticed by Catherine. During a rest point, she caught him alone, alongside a tree.

"Why have we left the trail, Mr. Fargo?"

"Defense tactics."

She studied him. "The Sioux?"

He nodded.

She shook her head. "This is one miserable trip, Mr. Fargo."

He smiled.

She caught the smile and bristled. "I suppose you want to say, 'I told you so.' "

"I wouldn't dare say it."

She looked away for a moment. "Well, you did tell us, I admit it. You said we'd be crazy to make this trip without the cavalry. I should have listened, I suppose."

"You'd miss all the fun," he said.

"Well, it's not been boring."

He looked at her sun-splashed light-blue eyes, her creamy skin, the curves of her body. What a misery that he had to think of fighting when he wanted playing.

"I've been a bit slow to say this, Fargo, but I suppose we'd never have gotten this far without you." Her smile was warm.

Damn, she was one beautiful woman, he thought.

"What do you think our chances are?" she asked.

His jaw hardened. "Red Sun and about fifteen Sioux mean lots of trouble."

She looked worried, then smiled. "I've come to have a lot of faith in you, Fargo."

It was nice, he thought, to feel her trust, something

new from her. In most situations, he could give her comfort, but not this one. Red Sun was his match, and maybe more, since this was his terrain and he'd pick the ground of combat.

"You've seen Red Sun. I'd rather have him with me than against me."

"Perhaps they'll let us go on our way," she said hopefully.

In a pig's eye, he thought, but smiled.

They reached the side of the mountain before the sun went down. The evening was calm, without incident, as he expected.

Still, he stayed close to the wagon, which he had positioned behind a giant boulder, just in case.

12

At midnight, he leaned against a boulder, looking up at a brilliant half-moon. The landscape in front of him, a mix of sloping hills, trees, and plateau, was clearly illuminated.

A peaceful enough moon, he thought, yet a declaration of war by the Sioux.

Nothing in the landscape looked worrisome, although a steep slope of ground could conceal a war party.

His wagon had fine protection, much better than the others.

For some reason Madden refused to take the attack seriously; he didn't believe the Sioux would dare to tackle white firepower. He had the guard duty for the morning, and Fargo stressed to him it would be the most dangerous time, to be sure everyone was out there, guns ready.

He wondered what the next twenty-four hours would bring. Death and destruction, the sort of thing Catherine complained seemed always to surround him. But by joining with the wagon train, he had cut down the odds of another Sioux massacre. Of course, they just might not attack; they might pick another time, another place.

It was time, for that matter, to get shut-eye; he'd give himself a wake-up signal before dawn. His bedroll was near the wagon, and though the women had retired hours ago, he could hear the murmur of their voices. It might be the same in the other wagons; fear was a great stimulant. He was himself not given to useless fear, but all these damned women kept his nerves on edge. And Red Sun was a deadly antagonist. Because he was on edge, he tossed the early part of the night, and fell into deep sleep toward the morning, so that it was the crack of gunfire that jarred him awake.

Instinctively, his hand grabbed for his rifle, and as he began to rise, trying to shake the thickness out of his mind, he looked around.

The sun was over the horizon, blazing into the camp, and the Sioux were racing hell-bent for leather from behind that ground slope, and yelling their brains out.

Jones and Clark were stumbling out of their wagons; Smitty and Madden were firing from their knees. He cursed himself for sleeping, then cursed Madden for not waking everyone.

He shifted two inches to the left, which put him behind the boulder. He heard Madden cry out, hit before he could reach cover, and he flipped about like a crazy doll before he fell. Clark, Smitty, and Jones were firing as fast as they could from their knees.

He peered over the boulder at the Sioux racing toward them, eight with rifles, the others with bows, some with flaming arrows, shooting at the wagons.

He sighted at a brave with a strip of hair down the middle of a bald skull, a face fiercely painted. His bullet hit the bull's-eye of his forehead and a bloody hole appeared; he rode like a sawdust figure before he fell. The second brave, with streaks of red and black on his face, was whipping his horse with his legs, his rifle firing. Fargo's bullet crashed into his chest, and he somersaulted over his horse and fell under the stomping hooves. A third had arched a burning arrow into a wagon when Fargo's bullet tore part of his skull off, and he fell in a whirl of arms and legs.

Fargo pulled back to look at the other men. Clark was dead, his neck shattered. Smitty was firing coolly. Jones had turned to see his wagon on fire, and the women and kids scrambling out, screaming. Bullets tore at them. Jones ran toward them, got hit, did a mad dance, and died.

The women and children were out of the burning wagons, running helter skelter, and a fusillade of bullets hit them from everywhere, especially from two Sioux dashing madly at them.

Fargo's pistols were out with lighting speed, spitting fire which catapulted them like twins out of their horses, crashing them to earth.

He turned: Smitty was dead, his body riddled with bullets.

It was Red Sun, on the far end, who did most of the damage, for he never wasted a shot. He rode a big sorrel, shooting from his rifle without sighting. He was shielded from Fargo's fire by a lean, muscled Sioux on a powerful black. Fargo slid his gun on the boulder, but a bullet splintered the stone in front of him. He dropped to his knees and peered out from the lower part of the boulder. He had a shot; he squeezed the trigger and the lean Sioux flung his arms wildly and plunged into the earth. Red Sun was visible for just a second, but again a bullet chipped the stone in front of him. When he could look out again there was a just the riderless sorrel. A black rock shaped like a domino on edge had to be Red Sun's cover.

Only two Sioux were left, driving hard, coming close: He could see their glaring eyes, their faces fierce with hate. He rolled to the other end of the boulder and came out laying down a curtain of lead. One leaped into the air, clawing it in a frenzy to reach him, then crawled and died. The other hugged tight against his horse, presented no target, using the body of the horse to conceal himself. As the hooves thundered by, he flung himself at Fargo, whose bullets caught him in the air, and his dead body hit the earth just inches away.

He fell back on his stomach, looked over the terrain. Nothing, just dead Sioux. Dead settlers. And smoking wagons.

And that rock, with Red Sun behind it.

Red Sun was pinned down, and so was he. It was a standoff.

For the first time, he looked back at his wagon. It stood there unscathed; the great boulder had done the trick.

Then he heard Catherine's voice. "Fargo?"

"Don't come out!" he warned. "Not till I tell you."

He looked at the other wagons. Burning. Silence. Men and women and children, sprawled in death. Nothing but the crackling of burning canvas and wood.

It was a wipeout.

He had positioned his wagon behind a great boulder,

beyond the reach of the burning arrows. And defended it against all comers.

All, no, not all. The most dangerous opponent of all, Red Sun, was still out there.

But they were all gone, Smitty, Madden, Clark, Jones, their families, and their dreams.

And the Sioux, all dead but Red Sun.

He crawled to the wagon and found the women white-faced. The cries, the screams, the firing, the smell of burning wagons made them feel the end was near. They had pistols in their hands, ready to shoot at the sign of a Sioux. But none came.

As long as they heard the bark of the guns, they knew he was alive. When everything went silent, they felt it would be the start of a nightmare.

It was then that Catherine called his name. When he answered, they felt joy. They told him this later.

In all this time, he kept an eye on the black rock. No movement. He reloaded his guns, took a swig of whiskey. Bit into leftover venison. Red Sun might be pinned down, but Fargo at least could eat and drink.

Catherine watched him eat, her eyes narrow.

"I don't know how you can be hungry at a time like this."

"Fighting sharpens the appetite," he said. He turned to Teresa. "Take this gun. If you see any movement, just shoot up in the air. Keep your eye on that black rock. Nowhere else."

"What happened out there?" asked Catherine.

"Everything happened."

"What do you mean?"

"There's nobody left, just me and Red Sun."

Her eyes widened.

"Nobody? None of the others? The women, the children?"

"All gone." His voice was flat.

They had come out here with great hopes, and it all came to an end on a barren spit of land near a mountain.

And it was not over yet.

Then came a small sound behind him, and his instinct came alive. He held up his hand for silence, threw a cup at the canvas, and a bullet ripped the canvas exactly where the cup had touched it.

He fired two shots, heard the scrambling, then a shot that sailed over his head kept him pinned down for a moment. He fired once more, then rushed to the side of the wagon to see Red Sun's leg disappearing behind a crag. He had made it into the mountain, and that would mean hell to pay.

Somehow Red Sun had managed to crawl flat as a pancake around the back of the wagon, completely unseen by Teresa, and made a try to bushwhack them. Only the gunfire had kept them all in one piece.

He thought deeply for a few moments, then cursed softly. There was no other way; he'd have to go in after Red Sun, and nobody could tell who would come out alive.

13

The passage into the mountain, where he stood, looking at Red Sun's prints, twisted up, crawled past crevices and caves, spiraled around giant crags; a place honeycombed with hideouts. To track Red Sun in that would be like tiptoeing on gunpowder.

He studied the prints thoughtfully. It would lock him up for hours to flush out Red Sun. And to go into that maze could be playing the game Red Sun wanted to play.

Fargo rubbed his jaw. Should he play? Perhaps he would, but there was time enough for killing. First he'd race the wagon the hell out of here, then run off all the horses. That would nail Red Sun down, for hours, at least. That damned sorrel might in the end find its master. But the main thing was to get the wagon and the women the hell out of this graveyard. The buzzards, sniffing a feast of death, had begun to swarm over the battlefield. He had to move fast.

When he got back into the wagon, the women looked jumpy.

"Listen," he said, "I'm going back in there. He's deep in the mountain, and it's gonna take time. So this is what you do. Hitch up the wagon and move fast to get back on the trail. I'll come later."

The women looked at each other, then at him.

"Why don't you just leave him up there?" Catherine said. "He may not follow us."

"Not follow us?" He grinned. "Fifteen of his brothers are dead out there. He's a Sioux. Do you think he's going to let us live?"

"There might be a chance," she said.

He shook his head. "Do you know what he'd say? 'The blood of my brothers is screaming from the earth for revenge.' " He sighed. "The earth talks to the Sioux." He looked at them. Their heads were bowed.

They hate the idea of traveling alone, he thought. Or maybe they were worried about him.

He rubbed his chin thoughtfully. "Red Sun is the kind of warrior who cannot accept the shame of defeat." He jerked his thumb at the ground littered with Indian corpses. "I think we can call that a defeat."

He looked out the wagon toward the trail. "Red Sun stands between us and Aberdeen like a mountain. If I go with you, he'll follow and hit us when he wants to. But if I stop him here, then you're on your way."

Catherine's light-blue eyes stared at him. "And if you don't stop him?"

"Then you're on your own." He grinned. "Keep your guns handy, all the time." He scratched his head. "Traveling to Aberdeen, Miss Catherine, wasn't exactly an excursion, was it?"

"I hate to think of you tangled with that terrible Indian," Elizabeth said suddenly. And she stepped forward, threw her arms around him, and kissed him. "Thank you, Fargo, for everything."

When she stepped back, Teresa, too, came forward, embraced him, and kissed him.

Their bodies, warm, soft, and female, felt great against his body. He looked at Catherine. "I have a lot of confidence in you. Keep the horses moving and just follow the trail."

Her blue eyes were glowing and strange. Then she stepped forward, like the others, pressed her body to him, and then her lips. Her body was just as he had imagined, a honey, with slender waist and full, firm breasts. Her lips were velvety against his, and the taste of her mouth was sweet. His body, hard against hers, felt a jolt of excitement.

As she pulled away, the skin of her face blushed pink.

"All right," she said, almost gruffly, to the others, "we've got a tough time ahead. And, as Fargo says, 'Let's move it!' "

Fargo grimaced as he slipped out of the wagon. She was all woman, dammit, and he had to leave it behind.

*   *   *

He took a soft step, froze, then stared at the prints going straight for the cavern. He had been using, for the last hour, just such a tactic—step and freeze, every nerve strained to catch sound or sight.

He was in a duel to the death with Red Sun, probably the most dangerous opponent in his life. To lose concentration even for a moment would be fatal.

They were on a flat bed of stone high in the mountain, and there were shoulders of rock on each side. A ten-foot column of rock towered behind him, and in front were Red Sun's prints tracked straight into the cavern.

Red Sun's strategy, up to now, had been to escape pursuit so that he could come from behind and attack. Once he had entered a mountain stream to come out later on the same side. He also scaled a twelve-foot rock with his hands, presenting the problem of disappeared footsteps.

At moments like these, the most dangerous, Fargo felt his skin crawl. He didn't know, at this moment, where Red Sun was, but Red Sun might know where Fargo was.

Now Red Sun, it seemed, had dropped the tricks and gone into the cavern. It looked like a simple cave, but if it had recesses in which to hide, it could be a hellhole.

By this time, Red Sun's eyes were adjusted to the dark, a terrific advantage.

Still, Fargo thought, it had to be a bad move, for it trapped the Sioux, unless it had an exit. He stood silent, looking at the mouth of the cave. It would be stupid for him to go in, his silhouette at the opening would give Red Sun the first shot. Fargo studied the ground. He could crawl forward and lay down a curtain of lead; all that was needed was one hit.

He went down to his stomach and began to crawl. Then, though he almost doubted his senses, he heard the sound, so soft it almost didn't reach him, but such a sound meant destruction. Even before his mind sorted out the meaning, he had wheeled and fired up. And he hit it, the only thing visible on the jutting column of rock behind him, the barrel of a rifle, which had been gently laid down on stone.

The velocity of his bullet crashing against the steel barrel tore it from Red Sun's hand, and the rifle skittered down the rock with a great clatter, slipping into a groove between the rock, to be lost forever.

He had him now, behind the columned rock. He made a rush to get up there, but it called for a climb of five massive rocks perched crazily on each other. And by the time he reached the top of the column, Red Sun had streaked down on the other side.

But now there was no hurry. Without his rifle Red Sun had lost some of his menace. But still, he should not be underestimated. He looked down at the prints leading to the cave. Red Sun, that red devil, had backtracked his prints to the stone column, climbed up, and just waited. Only the sound of the rifle touching stone just as he was about to blast had betrayed Red Sun.

Fargo, on top of the column, took a broad look before he started his pursuit. Above him, the spires of stone pointed at a cobalt sky laced with fleecy clouds. To the south, the mountain stretched out, vast, endless, the stone kneaded in fantastic forms.

But it would be just below him, in a gulley or a gorge, that he'd find Red Sun. The sooner the better. Three beautiful women, alone in a wagon on the trail, could only be a temptation to wild happenings.

He started his descent.

It took an hour of slow, agonized tracking over crags and into gullies to figure out what the Sioux was thinking. Red Sun had left the mountain, gone to the plateau, summoned his sorrel, and was heading south. South to the wagon! Of course. Not a moment to lose. With Red Sun's cunning, he could ambush the women and get the guns he needed to equalize the fight between them.

Fargo let out a volley of oaths at his stupidity, and whistled for the pinto. He heard the neigh even before the horse appeared, its eyes big and glittering, its nostrils flaring, as if it had detected a desperate urgency in the note of whistle.

He started the pinto off in a canter, to warm up those great muscles, then moved it into a gallop. The ears went back, the legs stretched out, and the hooves thundered against the earth. Red Sun had a start, it was true, but his sorrel could never keep pace with the pinto. And while the ground fled past, he again cursed himself for not figuring that Red Sun might pull a trick like this. Would he kill the women? He could, without batting an eye. His comrades were dead; the white man and his women had to pay.

He gritted his teeth and coaxed the horse to go all out. Not long after, he glimpsed the sorrel about a hundred yards in front of him, on the curve of the trail. He had not yet caught up with the wagon! He pulled his gun, but when he made the turn, Red Sun, aware of pursuit, had gone into a bypath, and was no longer visible. The bypath was thick with brush, trees. Perfect for ambush. So be it. Red Sun had no gun, but on terrain like this, his knife was just as deadly. And, further, this was his kind of fighting ground.

Under a darkening sky, he found himself in a tangled growth of bushes and trees without any idea of Red Sun's whereabouts. And, in spite of understanding how he had done it, climbing a tree, moving from branch to branch, Fargo had not been able to pick up his tracks. And in this darkened maze of trees, thick underbrush, it was unlikely that he would.

His gun was out, his ear was cocked, and his eyes studied the feature of every tree trunk, every branch. Dropping down off a tree was a favorite Indian trick. And because Red Sun had only his knife, his attack, if he made one, would have to come from close by. It was why, before he stepped under any tree, he examined it in detail. Soon it would be dark, something Red Sun probably was working for, since it would wipe out the edge given Fargo by his gun.

His jaw hardened as he gazed around. He had expected the Sioux to be tough to find, but not this tough. He had circled the terrain three times, studying everything, and he had seen practically no clue of Red Sun. He had seen prints at the foot of a huge tree, the one just passed. From there it was a mystery where he had gone. It seemed the earth had swallowed him up.

He froze.

The earth had swallowed him up!

His scalp crawled.

He had just passed, moments ago, a shallow grave.

Twice before his eye had casually picked it up; the recent grave of a Sioux buried quickly, he had thought.

That's exactly what it was! He whirled, his gun coming up, but already, it seemed, too late. Red Sun, rising like a ghost from the grave, had thrown his knife. It might have been the dirt in his eye, the darkened light, whatever, but the knife hit the wrist of Fargo's gun hand not with the point, but with the handle; it hit nerve and muscle, sent a paralyzing jolt to his arm, and the gun dropped.

Red Sun leaped up and threw himself at Fargo, his powerful hands reaching for the throat. Fargo by instinct crashed his left arm at those deadly hands, threw himself sideways. Red Sun, tipped off balance, came back in a crouch. Fargo, also in a crouch, circled, glad for the time to let feeling crawl back to his arm. Red Sun's eyes, in a hard glitter, looked as if he were facing a thing, not a man, a thing to be destroyed. Dirt stuck to his hair and eyebrows, and his great muscled body was coiled like a lion ready to jump. Fargo feinted, to keep him off balance, and crashed a right to the jaw, which jolted but did not hurt. Red Sun did not play the white man's game of fisticuffs; he made a headlong dive at Fargo, grabbing his legs, toppling him, and they rolled over and over, arms locking, each struggling for the death grip at the throat, but so equally matched that they countered each other's move. It went on and on, a frenzy of wrestling, grabs at legs, waist, head, the muscles of their bodies at utmost strain, aware this fight was to win or to die.

Fargo smelled the sweat of the Sioux, felt the dirt on his skin; he had dug that shallow grave with his knife, covered himself with earth, and waited patiently until he could hear Fargo pass by close enough. They disengaged, and as Fargo swung at the rib of the Sioux, he couldn't help admire that amazing trick, attacking not from above, but from below the ground. His loss of concentration proved costly, for Red Sun grabbed his arm and turned it, sending intolerable pain, as if it were coming out of the socket. He fell, his defense down for a split second, and Red Sun leaped astride him, hands grabbing for the throat. Fargo felt the sudden cutoff of oxygen, and soon darkness began to flood his brain, and looking into the eyes of Red Sun he saw his own death in them. The thought that all his life was to find its end here, like this, in this miserable patch of earth, seemed to release a gigantic surge of strength. Slowly, his hands pulled the hands of Red Sun from his throat, holding them while he gulped precious oxygen, and then, looking into the amazed eyes of Red Sun, he slowly pulled his arms wider. Then a quick rollover put him on top of the Sioux, and he began to crash his fist left and right at Red Sun's jaw. After eight blows the Indian's head went limp and his eyes closed.

Fargo stroked the smooth flank of the pinto, which always did a lot to calm it. It calmed him, too, for when you fight against someone trying to destroy you, only rage can give you the power to defend yourself.

And it had taken twenty minutes to leak the rage out of his system.

He looked down at Red Sun.

His face was bruised and swollen, but, Fargo thought, the Sioux had a lot to be grateful for—he was alive. He had tied the Sioux's hands, put him sitting against the trunk of the big tree. Red Sun had come to consciousness, and for the last five minutes his eyes, dull and empty, had followed Fargo's movements with the pinto.

He's in a shock of defeat, Fargo thought, and he sat down to look at the broad-boned face that somehow had lost its look of invincibility. He had lost in a one-to-one fight against the white man, and that, Fargo thought, meant if he was not dead, he deserved to die. That would be the code for a proud warrior like Red Sun.

They sat opposite, in silence, for a long time, then Red Sun spoke. "Why has Fargo not killed Red Sun?"

He drew a deep breath. "Fargo has no wish to kill his blood brother."

The dull eyes looked at him without interest. "Red Sun has lost in battle. He is ready to die."

"Fargo is not ready to kill."

Red Sun looked off into the distance. "The spirits of my fathers will wait for me."

Fargo smiled. "Let them wait."

"I have fought and lost. It is right for Red Sun to die."

"It is wrong for Red Sun to die," Fargo said.

The Indian, his face expressionless, said nothing.

"Life is good. Life can be good for Red Sun," Fargo said.

"It is finished." The Sioux's voice was flat.

Fargo pointed west. "The land is big. The land stretches far, out to the limits of the sky. The buffalo and the deer run there, they are many. It is good country for Red Sun."

The Sioux did not speak.

"Fargo asks Red Sun to forget revenge. Red Sun is given his life again. Let Red Sun go there, where the rivers run clear and the buffalo are many. There he will have sons and live in peace."

The Sioux's eyes gleamed, but still he did not speak.

Fargo studied him. He's too proud to take the offer of his life from a white man, he thought. He needs time, time to digest his humbled pride, time to see that I'm right. I'll leave him here with his knife stuck in the ground. By the time he gets loose, finds his sorrel, I'll be with the wagon. He rubbed his chin. But then, the riddle. What will he do? He's lost in a fair fight; he's been given his life. He's got a taste of the white man's mercy. And he's a man of honor—he's not going to hit the man who gave him his life.

Fargo got up, retrieved the knife thrown at him by Red Sun, and dug it into the earth in front of the Sioux. He looked deep into the brown eyes, put his hand to his heart, then turned toward the pinto.

The moon had been up two hours, giving good light, and the pinto had been riding hard before he caught up with the wagon. The women had made camp about twenty yards off the trail near a shelter of oaks. They had a stew cooking, and he picked up its delicious scent long before he got there. He became aware suddenly how hungry he was, especially for a hot meal. And how hungry he was for the sight of the female figure. They picked up the sound of his horse, and dropped flat to the ground, each with a pistol. He grinned. Before leaving he had drilled them in this act of self-defense.

"It's Fargo," he called.

"Fargo!"

There was jubilation in Teresa's voice.

They crowded around him as he unsaddled the pinto, rubbed its flank to show his love, and turned it loose for grazing.

Then he looked at them in the flickering light of the fire.

Catherine, Teresa, Elizabeth, three beautiful women, all smiling, ready to kiss him. He grinned. Like I'm the victor home from the wars, he thought. What the hell, I am.

Teresa kissed him hard, pressing against his body.

Elizabeth did the same, the flesh pressing, and by that time, his own flesh was pressing back. In fact, it was jumping, which Catherine, with the antennae of women, picked up. It may have been why she leaned forward just to peck his cheek, clearly timid about possibly rousing a sleeping giant.

"Damn, I'm hungry," he said, and he didn't suppose it necessary to add for more than just a good stew.

It was Elizabeth who spooned the stew into his tin dish. "Fighting sharpens the appetite." She smiled.

"Hell, yes." And his eyes went hard over her breasts.

Teresa and Elizabeth laughed.

"Let us suppose you mean food," said Catherine. "And I hope you'll tell us what happened."

"We were terribly worried," Teresa said.

"We feared for your life," said Elizabeth. "That Indian looked unbeatable."

"Did you kill him?" asked Teresa, her eyes glowing.

He forked the stew into his mouth. It was a mix of beef, potatoes, onions, and herbs, and damned good.

They watched him eat, waiting for him to talk.

"Well?" Catherine asked.

"No," he said. "I didn't kill him."

They stared.

"I just couldn't." The silence was long and meaningful. "I gave him a choice. Told him to go to the west. To live long and have sons."

"That was generous," Teresa said, smiling.

"Yes," said Elizabeth.

Catherine did not smile. "It was too generous. Are you

saying you defeated him in a fight, then simply told him to go west?"

He nodded. That starchy teacher; everything had to be clear for her.

"What did he say?"

Fargo looked at the fire. There were some things women couldn't understand. Could it be explained?

"He's a Sioux. He's proud. A great warrior. He's not going to say, 'Thanks a lot, I'm on my way.' He has his pride, his manhood."

Catherine looked at the other women. "All that male nonsense."

He frowned. There was a gap between men and women, he thought; there were some things hard to be made clear to women at all.

"So now," Catherine said, "we have a very dangerous Indian who *may* go west." She paused. "Unless he decides not to."

"You don't understand these things. I beat him. Then I gave him his life. Now it's a thing of honor. Men who fight know about these things."

She shook her head. "Men think they know a lot of things. But I won't argue." She paused. "It's just that what you thought was a generous act has put us all in danger."

He rubbed his chin. Could that be true? If he had killed Red Sun, yes, it would have wiped out all risk. And, when you came down to it, did he have the right to put the women in danger? A dead Red Sun couldn't hurt them. A live one could rip the hell out of things, commit rape and massacre. Why had he spared the most dangerous Sioux of them all? Well, you didn't destroy a man like Red Sun easily. It would be like killing a lion, a magnificent lion.

He scratched his armpit. I'm counting on Red Sun, that he's got a noble streak, he thought. But still it was chancy. Red Sun might think he owed more to his people than to a white man who had spared his life. He might think that; then what? It was a riddle. You just make a decision and hope you were right.

"You just make a decision," he said, voicing his thought.

She had been watching him. "All right, Fargo. Eat your stew. I tend to worry a lot. What happens will happen."

He nodded, "I agree, Miss Catherine, you worry a lot. But you're one smart lady."

He put a spoonful of stew in his mouth.

"Damn, this is good," he said and grinned.

They all smiled at him.

He sat up, feeling restless, the leaves of the oak above his head quivered in the light, grass-scented breeze. He could hear the sounds of the summer night: the hum of insects, the cry of a nighthawk, the howl of a coyote. The moon had arched high over head, and its light silvered the earth. He suddenly realized he had been dreaming, a hot dream, and dammit, of all women, it had to be of Catherine, the one beauty he had the least chance of bedding down. But in his dream, he had stumbled on her coming out of a stream, naked as a jay, with full ripe breasts. And she came toward him, stopped in front of him, all silky and creamy. "Fargo," she said, "I can't fight it anymore. I must have you." And she flung herself on his body in a rage of desire, and they had reached a pitch of passion, and he was just on the verge of reaching into the depths of her when he awoke.

Must have been that hot stew, he thought. But then, he had been primed for sex, and he felt frustrated about the dream's being torn off at that torchy moment. It was a damned shame he couldn't get the real thing, and he wondered why Elizabeth or Teresa had not come out to play.

For that matter, why, dammit, had he waked up?

He stiffened.

Usually, he waked up on the trail only because that alarm instinct deep in his brain had picked up something.

His eyes narrowed, and he slowly moved his head and listened.

Nothing. But something was bothering him. He didn't yet know what.

He stood up and stretched. There was something wrong in the camp; he sensed it, and he had learned long ago never to ignore the warnings from the depths of his mind.

He studied the tree trunks, the thickets, the branches, the wagon. He moved toward the wagon. The women sleeping in it were quiet. The silence in the camp was almost deafening, but still he felt uneasy. Could it be that all the talk about Red Sun had left him nerved up? If you went to sleep with troubling thoughts, they would wake you deep in the night. Most probably that explained it. He had bad thoughts and they gave insomnia. But he would make sure. If there was anything wrong, it might be a drifter, a prowling animal, anything. He moved slowly, with soft steps, his eyes studying the great shadows. He went past the wagon, listened to the breathing of the women, then moved to the horses.

He felt odd. His senses told him the camp was secure, but his instinct left him edgy.

Prowling brought him back to the wagon, where he stood, still uneasy. He stood absolutely quiet.

Then he held his breath. Pulled his gun.

Something, something, made him look under the wagon.

There! He looked into the glaring eyes of Red Sun, hanging over the axle, holding in his hand a lance that he had made, ready for a thrust.

Even as Fargo's body mobilized, bringing up his gun hand, Red Sun struck out with the lance, hitting his arm with such force his hand went nerveless and the gun dropped. Red Sun scrambled forward, thrusting the lance, forcing Fargo to whirl back. He stumbled to the ground, and Red Sun leaped forward, struck again. Fargo twisted away; the lance pierced the ground two inches from his body. Fargo grabbed the lance with one hand. Red Sun jerked it back, then jerked again with more force; Fargo let go, and as Red Sun tumbled back, Fargo jumped forward. Red Sun stopped him with both feet and kicked, hurling Fargo back and spinning. Now they crouched and circled each other; Red Sun thrust right, then left, missing by inches. Fargo grabbed the lance at the third thrust, feeling the return of strength in his right hand. He moved in on the lance, looking deep into the eyes of Red Sun.

"You fool," he hissed.

The eyes did not change, and Fargo knew it was a fight to the death, red man against white, a killing game, by fair means or foul.

The Sioux tugged hard at the lance, and Fargo suddenly let go; the Sioux stumbled, and Fargo leaped forward, ducking under the lance, butting his head against the chest of the Sioux, who went down. Fargo sprawled over him, clubbing the forearm holding the lance. He hit it over and over with his fist until the fingers uncurled and the lance dropped. Fargo leaped up, kicked at the lance, rolling it out of reach, then turned to face Red Sun, saw the moonlight glittering cruelly on steel as Red Sun rushed, the knife upraised. Fargo danced right, and the knife missed his body by an inch. Red Sun struck again as Fargo danced left, another near miss. Red Sun, his eyes glittering, his face cold fury, turned the knife, holding it by the blade to throw. Fargo dropped, scooped dirt, threw it at the Sioux's eyes, and leaped, hurtling into the Indian. Red Sun fell, sprawling, and Fargo was astride him at once. But the Sioux managed to turn the knife so that again he held the handle and tried to strike upward. Fargo grabbed the wrist with his own hand. Red Sun's muscled arm tried to push up. Fargo pushed down, and their movement looked frozen, like the statues of men in a death battle. Then Fargo brought his head close to the deadly hand, sank his teeth into the wrist, felt the blood spurt into his mouth. The knife dropped; with a lightning move, he grabbed it, thrust it into Red Sun's chest. It slipped in like slicing into butter. Red Sun's body quivered, his eyes locked on Fargo's; the look in them went from hate, to puzzlement, finally to serenity. Bright-red blood spurted from the wound. Fargo, watching Red Sun dying, felt a rush of melancholy.

The waste, the waste!

He reached for the limp hand, held it; then, at last, he felt the small, answering pressure, as if dying, Red Sun had saluted the bond between then, a bond that went beyond the battle between the red man and the white man.

When the light in Red Sun's eyes died, Fargo closed them, then stood up.

It was then that he saw the women.

They were standing in their pantalettes, each holding a pistol she dared not fire, from the fear of hitting him.

14

He looked at the mound over Red Sun's body and bowed his head. The women, standing at the wagon, watched in silence, respecting his feelings.

For them, he realized, the Indian was an enemy who had just come to kill. They didn't understand.

Two bluejays chirping loudly swooped by; the sun glowed as it started its climb up on a slate-blue sky; dew sparkled on the blades of grass. The land stretched out vast, fertile, beautiful.

Fargo took Red Sun's lance and dug it into the head of the grave. Last night it had been a wicked weapon of death in the hands of Red Sun.

Fargo stood silently, with bowed head, thinking. Red Sun had come the second time to fight because he could not take the idea of defeat. Defeat meant bondage, and Red Sun would rather be dead.

He had the spirit of a mighty eagle who would die in captivity.

Fargo picked up some earth, threw it at the grave.

"Dust to dust," he muttered.

The wagon rolled again and the land turned lush, stretches of green, with sprawling great oaks, wayside daisies, pansies, violets.

In the early afternoon they passed a great wagon train that had stopped for lunch. They waved at the busy settlers, the yelling youngsters, and the stern-faced troopers who looked curiously at them.

That night, when they stopped to make camp, Fargo told them it would be the last night on the trail. By noon tomorrow, they'd be in Aberdeen.

During the afternoon, he had sighted a duck on the

wing, and brought it down with a single shot. The women put it on a spit over fire, and they had roasted duck flavored with herbs that Catherine had collected on the trail.

Afterward, they sat around the fire sipping coffee, and for the first time, Fargo felt they were justified in feeling safe. They would be in Aberdeen tomorrow, and the mood was sprightly.

"I'll be so glad to get out of this gray uniform," Teresa said, brushing her red hair.

"Me, too," said Elizabeth, her dark eyes flirting with Fargo.

"I suppose we all will," said Catherine. "The trouble with wearing a nun's habit is it makes you try to be a bit saintly."

"And that's a damned shame," Fargo said. "You should try to remember that you are three beautiful, full-blooded women." He grinned. "With the needs of such women."

"Trust Fargo to jog our memories about that," Elizabeth said, with a quick smile.

Catherine stretched. "I can't wait to get to Aberdeen. Back to a civilized life. Where you can go to sleep and not wake up to find yourself scalped."

"Oh, lordy," said Elizabeth. "That terrible Red Sun. There must have been at least five times last night when I thought you'd be killed. He was so quick, so deadly."

"But Fargo was deadlier," Teresa said. "I kept looking for a chance to shoot, but you both moved so quickly, I was sure I'd hit you, instead."

"Good thing you didn't shoot," he growled. "You might have made me a eunuch."

The thought of Red Sun shifted his mood, and he lifted his coffee cup, feeling pensive. "It was bad about Red Sun," he said aloud.

Catherine frowned. "I'm afraid, Fargo, I don't share your concern about the Indian. Like other Indians, all he seemed to want was to scalp you and rape us. He led that charge against the settlers. It destroyed them all."

He stared at her, then felt a wild rush of anger. "You don't know anything about it, lady. All you've done this trip is wag your tongue and find fault. Preachy little schoolmarm! What do you know about a man like Red Sun?"

She was startled at his attack and looked hurt. She almost turned away. He had come down on her like a ton of bricks.

Everyone was silent.

"I'm sorry, Mr. Fargo," she said, "if I've hurt your feelings. I was expressing my honest view. It's hard to feel good about someone who wants to kill you. And he did try that, even after you gave him a chance to live."

Now he felt he had hit her too hard, unjustly. She saw it from a woman's view, and, after all, Red Sun had come after them.

They watched him sip his coffee.

Then he felt a wave of feeling, and his throat tightened.

He spoke. "He was an Indian. He loved his land. He loved to live free, to hunt and fish, to ride his range. Like a man. This is the way his fathers lived. Then we come, we, the white man. We kill his buffalo, and not for food. We grab his land, we kill his squaw, his children. What should he do? What would any man do? He'd fight, fight without mercy to stop the intruder. To be terrible, so they would fear to come. To destroy, and if he could not destroy them, he would die fighting, because he had too noble a spirit to live in a world that would not let him live free. That was Red Sun. A man. A man."

There was a long silence.

Then Teresa came over, kissed his cheek, and went to the wagon.

Elizabeth did the same.

Catherine stood there. "I'm sorry, Fargo. I think I understand now."

He smiled. "It's all right. No damage done. This time tomorrow, you'll be looking over your schoolroom."

"Yes, it's a happy thought." Then her blue eyes deepened. "No more adventures on the trail, no more Indian raids. Just the dull, deadly routine of teaching naughty little brats how to read. No more fights with Fargo." She paused. "No more fun."

"No—no more fun," he said. They looked at each other, and damned if he didn't feel a wave of melancholy.

*　　*　　*

Fargo leaned back in his bedroll, hands locked behind his head, and looked up. The sky glittered with a million silver chips on a great coat of dark blue. The scent of flowers hit his nostrils, and an owl hooted from a nearby oak.

A summer night in a beautiful land. His stomach felt good, nourished by the dinner of duck and spuds.

Everything seemed to be falling into place.

He had brought the women and their wagon unscathed through a corner of hell. Not a hair on their head had been touched, although rape and massacre had seemed only a hairbreath away.

He heaved a deep breath. Now that the neighborhood did not threaten death and destruction, he became aware of his body. It would be nice, he thought, on this last night before Aberdeen to enjoy a slight touch of rape.

Teresa, that hot-blooded redhead, during dinner had slipped him a wicked wink, and it made him aware that he had the lust up for the body of a woman.

Lying there only in his shorts, he looked down at his body, aware that he was muscled all over, even at his groin.

He was, in other words, horny as hell, and figured it would be a restless night if Teresa did not appear and bring along her beautiful body.

He squirmed restlessly.

The women slept spread out, one in the wagon, the others near it. He couldn't very well tiptoe over to Teresa and carry her off.

He ground his teeth in frustration.

Tomorrow they'd be in Aberdeen, and there he was counting on taking care of his business with Clay. He had made Aberdeen his destination only because of his hope for a showdown with Clay.

But he'd not think of Clay now; there would be time enough when he reached Aberdeen.

He leaned back, listened to the mournful hoot of the owl, turned restlessly, and ground his teeth.

He was horny as a polecat, and if Teresa did not appear, he could bore a gopher hole in the bedroll.

Time slipped by, the moon swung overhead, his lids started to go leaden, and he drifted into uneasy sleep.

He was heavy with sleep when he felt light fingertips on his chest.

He smiled in his sleep, started up from the depths. She had come, finally; it would have been a crime to let this last night on the trail get away without one last pitch in the passion pit.

Eyes still closed, he reached for the warm body close to him. His hands touched a plump breast.

"Teresa," he murmured dreamily.

A sharp gasp.

"Oh!"

Then a slap across his face, which snapped his eyes wide open.

Catherine!

She scowled at him, jumped up, and started to race off.

He came to life in a split second and with a quick leap, caught her arm, swung her about.

He looked down into her face.

Her light-blue eyes looked stormy. But that beautiful face with its full lips, and that lush blond hair, and the deep breasts!

"Wait," he said.

Her mouth firmed. "Wait for who? Teresa? Why not? You can let me go."

"Oh, no!" he said. "Not you!"

She looked a bit mollified at the intensity of his voice.

"I don't want to disappoint you, Fargo. If you've been dreaming of Teresa. I'm sure it can be arranged."

He smiled. "Catherine, in my dreaming I've thought about you. But I never expected you to really happen."

The storm went out of her eyes. "That's better."

He led her back, and she didn't resist. He felt a hell of a pulsebeat. Catherine, all blond and beautiful, maybe on the verge of a hayride, oh, happy day!

"Why didn't you come earlier?" he asked, as she sat down on the bedroll.

"Oh, I felt your appeal, Fargo. I suppose all women do. But I resisted it."

"I wish you hadn't."

She seemed a bit embarrassed by the way he looked at her. "Your fight with the Indian. It was terrifying. I thought you'd never escape. My skin was crawling with fear."

"You didn't want to lose me?"

Her eyes sparked. "No, Fargo, we don't want to lose you." She smiled. "The girls wouldn't like that much."

He laughed and pulled her to him.

Her breast was against his chest, her body pressed against him.

His flesh was already in excitement, she felt the strength of him against her. Her eyes glowed, her lips went half open.

He bent to kiss her, and her mouth was soft, sweet-tasting. They kissed again and again.

His hands snapped down the top of her pantalettes, and the full white breasts jutted out, their pink nipples erect. He nuzzled his face against the silky skin, ran his tongue in a circle over the tip of one, holding the creamy softness of the other.

He could hear the sharp intake of her breath. He kept at it, delighting in their delicacy, fullness, then, with a quick movement, he pulled down on her pantalettes, and she stepped deftly out of them.

Nude, she was a feast, with a figure put together by a master designer, her body curving from the ripe breasts to a slender waist, arching to womanly hips, faultlessly shaped thighs with an exquisite blond triangle. He stroked the line of her breasts, her hips, her buttocks, astonished at the silky sheen of her white skin. His hand went to the tempting triangle; he stroked it delicately, and she quivered, he probed into the velvet warmth; her breath came hard and fast. Then he dropped to the blondness of her, put his lips there, and the magic of it soon made her moan, again and again.

"Oh, oh," she breathed.

He slipped out of his shorts, and she grasped his maleness, awed by its fierceness; she dropped to her knees, caressing, kissing, her mouth giving endless tribute.

He then put her down on the bedroll, and her legs opened to his probing, he felt the silken flesh part and went into the lush warmth, feeling her tightness about his enormous cock.

He looked down at her face. She seemed to be in a trance of pleasure.

He started slowly, and soon her pelvis picked up his rhythm, each movement engulfing him, the tightness giving each stroke great rippling pleasure.

Suddenly, she went taut, and her body heaved with intense sensations.

He paused, then again picked up his rhythm, and again it happened, the tightening of her whole body, a sharp intake of breath, a moan, as of intolerable pain. He went on, holding her, feeling his own pleasure climbing to a ferocious intensity. Then it all came together, an intolerable pitch of feeling; it stayed high, then he surged, and she flung herself against him, violently, as if trying to merge the flesh of her body into his.

For a scalding moment they stayed like that, then he loosened her. They held each other until the world around them began to appear.

He looked down at her and grinned.

Her eyes were blurred and teary, and she looked as if she'd had the ride of her life.

15

They were on the outskirts of Aberdeen and Fargo was trotting the pinto alongside the wagon when the two saddle bums came thundering up. They stopped, looked at the wagon, then at Fargo.

"Staying over at Aberdeen?" The saddle bum wore a red kerchief and a brown hat; his small ratlike eyes moved furtively from the women to Fargo. His sidekick looked impatient to move on.

"Maybe." Fargo didn't care for the smell of them, but they seemed harmless. "Any good lodgings for the women in town?" he asked. The women had changed into Levi's and cotton shirts.

"The Alcott, best hotel in town," rat-eyes said, and he tipped his hat at the women. "Where you folks coming from?"

Fargo's eyes gleamed. He didn't like to answer such questions. "You men know Aberdeen?"

"Like the palm of my hand. They call me Slick." He smirked and looked at the women, fascinated by them.

"Know a man called Clay?"

A flicker of the eyes, then a look of caution. "Seems like I heard the name. You got business with him, mister?"

Fargo's eyes were hard. "Yes. Business with him."

There was a heavy silence, then the men looked at each other.

Then Slick spoke. "What's it about? If we run into him, we'll tell him."

Fargo thought suddenly of Lily, and he couldn't help feel a shot of intense rage.

"I want to give him regards from a friend."

Slick's eyes glinted with cunning, and he tried to talk casually. "Who shall I say is looking for him?"

Fargo gave him a slow hard smile.

"Just someone who wants to meet him."

The other rider, impatient, spoke. "If we see Mr. Clay, we'll tell him."

They tipped their hats to the women, and with a whoop they took off, galloping their horses.

Fargo watched until they disappeared around a turn in the trail. That bastard Clay *was* in Aberdeen! That gave him a lift. His whole trip, through fire and fury, had actually been for one aim: Clay. And it was clear that these mangy saddle bums knew Clay; they looked the type.

Then he thought again about Lily, the way they had found her, the way she had been degraded and destroyed. And his rage started up again.

Catherine, seeing him in a deep study, called, "Fargo, what are you dreaming about? Are you forgetting us, now that we're almost in Aberdeen?"

He looked at her and at the others, then grinned. "I'm not likely to forget any of you. Not likely. Ever."

The women looked at each other and smiled broadly.

Teresa spoke in a low voice, which floated out to him.

"We're not likely to forget you either. Ever."

They all laughed.

He started to grin, but the thought of Clay flashed back to his mind, and all he could feel was the rage that again seemed to saturate every part of his body.

Fargo walked down the main street of Aberdeen, toward Dugan's Saloon and Dance Hall. A man like Clay, who liked the smell of whiskey, women, and gambling, would find his way to Pete's.

Fargo's eyes moved restlessly, scrutinizing every man on the street, on the porches, every rider on horseback. They were hard-faced men, wranglers, rustlers, gamblers, hunters, drifters. Almost all wore guns. He looked hard at them, and they, in turn, looked curiously at him. The size and look of him made them wary. He passed a plate-glass window and caught his reflection: big, lean, tough, and fast. Most men in towns always gave him plenty of space.

Since his last visit, Aberdeen had grown surprisingly.

More settlers, more stores, more houses, more women of easy virtue. The town was beginning to sprawl. It was half wild, half respectable.

He had taken the women up to the Alcott Hotel and put them in the charge of the school principal, Stuart Fremont, a sedate gentleman who looked extremely pleased about his new teachers.

"I have to look up an old friend," he told Catherine, after they were settled in. Each of the women kissed him before he left. Catherine's embrace was especially intense. Since their love games of the night before, she had done a turnabout in her attitude, and for the rest of the trip into Aberdeen, she was like pure honey. It proved to him, once again, that nothing sweetened a woman more than a night of loving. If a man could love his woman every hour on the hour, he'd probably have him the sweetest missy in the world.

Pity, he thought, that most men didn't actually have the strength.

Such thoughts drifted through his mind as he walked toward the saloon.

He stared at the hard-faced men, looking for one in particular, a man with flat black hat and black shirt, a broad face with a slit of a mouth, and perhaps scars on the right cheek, a reminder from Lily Baines.

He had never seen Clay, but it would take just a moment for recognition.

He looked at the ferret-eyed drifter coming toward him. Everything about him was furtive, crooked, the sort who'd shoot a man in the back for his boots. You saw such scurvy faces in towns like Aberdeen, but rarely on the trail. It was why he enjoyed being out there most of his days in God's own clean world. But he was in Aberdeen to do a job, and he'd better get on about it.

Then he saw the man named Slick. He was leaning on a railing in front of the watering trough, and next to him was a huge ox of a man, with big shoulders, bone-crushing hands, a broad face under a huge Stetson. He looked as if he might be the strong man in a circus, and his bright brown eyes in the broad-boned face were fastened on Fargo. Slick said a few words in his big ear, and he nodded and smiled.

Not a nice smile, thought Fargo, who sensed an ugly diversion and that he would have to do whatever he could not to let that happen.

"Hey," the big man called as Fargo came abreast.

Fargo pretended not to hear and kept walking. The voice was deep-throated and harsh. "Hey, you, shorty."

Fargo felt an impulse to laugh, but instead, he turned to look around, as if somebody else were being called. Then he looked into the bloodshot brown eyes. "I mean you," said the harsh voice. The big man was leaning against the wooden rail. There were four men behind him, townsfolk, idle onlookers at anything taking place in the street.

Fargo walked over.

Fargo was tall, but this ox was at least a head taller, and he looked brick-hard. His voice seemed to come from a cavern in his chest. He poked a finger at Slick.

"Slick tells me you're lookng for Mr. Clay. What's it about, Shorty?"

Again, Fargo felt the impulse to laugh. No one in his life had ever dreamed of calling him Shorty. "Whatever it's about is none of your business," he said.

"I told you he'd be snotty, Bigfoot," Slick said.

Bigfoot frowned. He's not used to taking guff, Fargo thought. Small wonder; he had hands like hams. Then, for the first time, Fargo noticed that he was not wearing a gun.

Bigfoot's bloodshot eyes were examining him carefully; he nodded as if he liked what he saw.

"You should be more respectful, Shorty. Clay ain't in town just now. He's expected back tonight. He's a busy man. And he likes to know who he's dealing with. So what's your business with him?"

"My business, Bigfoot, is with Clay. Nobody else."

Bigfoot's mouth tightened. "What's your handle, mister?"

"The name's Fargo."

There was a moment's silence. "Fargo, huh?" Bigfoot squinted.

Slick's eyes widened. "He's the Trailsman."

Bigfoot nodded. "Yeah, Fargo, we've heard of you. So, I'm asking, what's your business with Clay?"

"That's my business, Bigfoot."

"You ain't polite, mister." Bigfoot rubbed his massive jaw.

Fargo smiled. "Well, I wouldn't invite you to my tea party, either."

The men at the railing laughed, but they stopped when Bigfoot stared at them.

Bigfoot then began to roll up his shirtsleeves. "You got a big rep with a gun, Fargo. But I'm not wearing one. Why don't you take yours off? You need to be taught a lesson."

Fargo hesitated. This big galoot could break a lot of bones, put him out of action for Clay tonight. He'd have to back off.

"I've no quarrel with you, Bigfoot. Just let me go my way."

Bigfoot stretched lazily, and the muscles of his biceps swelled and rippled. He looked as if he could knock down a buffalo with the swing of his fist.

"Well, Fargo, I got a quarrel with you. I don't like your manners. I'm gonna improve them, teach you to be a nice, agreeable fella." He took a step toward Fargo.

Fargo turned his back and started to walk.

"Fargo!" He heard Slick's voice, sharp, threatening. He turned. Slick had his gun out.

"Drop your gunbelt, Fargo."

Fargo took a deep breath. It was a setup, of course. He loosened his gunbelt and looked at Bigfoot. He had a jaw like iron, great shoulders and arms, hard chest, but his gut didn't look all that hard. Of course, if Bigfoot landed one clean punch, it might be all over, but he had to get past this bully who stood in his way.

"I'm not asking for a fight, Bigfoot. You're forcing my hand." He moved in, crouching, his fists cocked.

"That's all right, Fargo, I'll put you to sleep quick." And he swung a monstrous fist at Fargo, who nimbly stepped aside. He's not going to hit me square unless I get careless, Fargo thought. And then he threw a hard fist at Bigfoot's jaw. His hand clear up to his elbow jarred; it was an iron jaw, just as he had thought.

Bigfoot grinned, then made a surprisingly fast swing that managed to hit his arm. The jolt made him aware that he had to stay clear and stay light-footed; if this monster connected, he might tear his head off. He drove a powerful right at Bigfoot's ribs. Bigfoot flinched. He didn't like that. Fargo moved lightly to the left, swung a powerhouse at the left ribs. Bigfoot growled and rushed. Fargo stepped aside, drove a right to his gut, felt his fist sink in. Bigfoot blenched. He didn't like that either, and he rushed, swinging wild power blows. Fargo weaved from side to side, staying clear of the flying hammer fists, but one grazed the side of his head and he felt it down to his toes. He stood petrified a moment, and Bigfoot grabbed his body, folded it in his arms, and gave the grizzly hug. Fargo lost his breath, felt his back near breaking. He put his middle fingers under Bigfoot's nostrils and thrust up with all his might. He felt the blood flow over his fingers. Bigfoot's grasp loosened, and Fargo, with his knuckle out, slammed his fist into the right eye. Bigfoot let out a roar that almost stampeded the tied-up horses at the railing, and reached for his eye.

Fargo pulled back while Bigfoot looked at the blood in his palm, flowing from his nose. His right eye was starting to swell. He roared again and rushed at Fargo, who sidestepped, waiting to get back breath and strength. Bigfoot stopped, rubbed his eye, and rushed again at Fargo, who sidestepped, but crouching this time and crashing a right to the gut. Bigfoot grunted, stumbled, and came back in a scramble, and Fargo again drove at the right rib. In a blind rage, Bigfoot wheeled and with astonishing speed grabbed at Fargo, caught his arm, held him, then grabbed his body, raised him as if he were a bag of rags, and flung him at the wooden corner post of the building. Fargo twisted in the air and missed the post by inches, landing on his hands and knees. Still, it knocked the wind out of him, and Bigfoot rushed up and kicked at his ribs. Only a slight turn of his body saved Fargo from that great boot which would have crushed every bone in his rib cage. Even so, he felt a sharp pain. Bigfoot threw himself at Fargo's prone body, but Fargo twisted and rolled away. He got to his feet, foggy in his head. He needed time for his head to clear, and he squirmed away from the great hamlike hands grabbing at him. He kept moving while Bigfoot kept rushing. Fargo felt himself slowing down, which could be fatal; any one of Bigfoot's monster swings could destroy him if they landed clean. Fargo kept moving, though he hurt all over. He looked at Bigfoot's swollen, enraged face; now the right eye was completely closed. If only he could get the other. There was no way of knocking out this monster without killing him, his head was stone, his jaw iron, and he was strong as a grizzly. The left eye, the left eye! He danced to the left, let Bigfoot swing a blow that missed by inches, balanced his weight, and swung at the eye, putting all the force of his shoulder and back into the punch. He felt the crunch, as if a grape had been crushed. Bigfoot let out a howl of pain, clapped his hand to his eye, then, as if suddenly blind, reached around, grabbing wildly with his hands with the hope of nailing Fargo. Blood poured from the eye, and he looked like a blind Samson, grabbing with fury at the empty air.

"Where are you, you bastard, Fargo, where, where?" And in his frustration and fury, because he could not see, he stopped, then dropped to the ground, held his eyes.

"Slick, Slick," he said finally.

Fargo picked up his gunbelt and strapped it on. He felt as if he had been put through a wrecking machine. His body ached from top to toe. He put his hat back on.

He looked around, then became aware that the street was filled with people. They had poured out of the buildings from everywhere.

They were looking at him, almost with awe. Then one old-timer said, "That's the greatest fight I ever saw." Then somebody cheered, then they all joined in, a giant roar as if from one throat.

Fargo looked at them, tipped his hat, then moved painfully back toward his hotel. He went into his room, washed his face and body, then lay down on the bed. He got up, locked his door, then lay down again, and slept for four hours.

16

He opened his eyes, moved, felt the ache in every part of his body. Damn, he thought, if I move too quick, I'll break like glass. During the fight with Bigfoot he had managed to avoid a direct punch from those great ham fists, but still he felt wrecked.

He stretched with care, grateful that he had no broken bones, moved slowly to loosen his muscles, then got up and shuffled to the window. The sun was halfway down the sky, and he realized with a shock how long he had slept.

He thought of the women, and it mystified him why they had not looked in on him. They had not seen the fight, of course, they must be out with the principal on school business. Anyway, his door had been locked and he had probably slept through everything.

His gut growled, and he realized how much he needed food. He clattered downstairs to the hotel dining room, where a grinning boy of about sixteen was setting tables. He ordered two steaks, candied yams, black-eyed peas, and corn.

He wolfed it all down, then ate a piece of pecan pie and drank two cups of coffee. Then he came alive, looked more carefully at the waiter, a stripling who had watched him eat with eyes like saucers.

Now with his gut full, his blood singing in his veins, he was willing to take note of the world.

"Whatcha grinning about, small fry?"

"Never saw anyone eat that fast, Mr. Fargo."

"You should catch me when I'm hungry, boy." Fargo lit a cheroot and blew smoke at the ceiling. He felt human again, felt his reflexes had come back.

"I saw you," the boy said.

"Saw what?"

"Saw your fight. Nobody in this town ever stopped Bigfoot. You did it." He grinned.

Fargo rubbed his arm; it still hurt. "Hey, boy, where are the ladies I brought here? Did they eat?"

The boy shook his head. "They left."

"Left?" He frowned. "When?"

"About an hour ago. They left with Slick Carson."

Fargo, about to sip coffee, froze. He stared at the boy, put down the cup, and went bounding upstairs to the rooms given to the women. Empty, clothing scattered on the beds, powder spilled. A rush exit, obviously.

He looked out the back window. The wagon was gone.

He tore down the stairs to the desk, where the clerk, a thin bald man, was pushing papers.

"Hey, did you see those three ladies leave?"

The clerk frowned, and his thin lips pressed tight. "Yes, Mr. Fargo, I did."

"With who?"

"Slick Carson, and a sidekick."

"Why didn't somebody stop them?"

"Stop them?" Baldy stared. "Those men are in the Clay bunch. You don't fool with men like that. Besides, we didn't know but what the women had something to do with them."

"Was Clay with them?"

"No." He turned to one of the boxes. "They left an envelope for you."

Fargo glared at him. "Why didn't you wake me?"

Baldy shrugged. "They told us not to. But we did try, later. Your door was locked."

Fargo tore the letter open. The words were scribbled in pencil:

Just keep moving, Fargo, and get out of town. And nothing will happen to the women. But if you try and make trouble, what happens will be your fault.

Clay

Fargo read the note twice, and when he reached the last line, the anger went through him like scalding steam.

His pinto had needed a bit of shoe work, so he had left

it with Dixon, the smith, a man he knew and liked. When he walked into the smith, Dixon took one look at him and brought the pinto out.

"I know when a man's in a hurry."

Fargo threw the saddle over the horse and tightened the cinches. Then he looked at Dixon. "Do you know Clay?"

Dixon nodded. "Ask if I know the devil?"

"Does he have a spread near town?"

"Just south of town. Not a spread, a house, a hideaway on Skytop Hill. Not easy to get up there."

Fargo swung over the pinto and threw a golden eagle at Dixon, who caught it and grinned.

"He's fast with a gun, Fargo. Half crazy. And shrewd. He doesn't stick his neck out."

Fargo scowled. "If he's so fast, why is he on the run?"

"Is he on the run?" Dixon thought a moment. "Well, Fargo, you've got a rep with the gun. I told you he's shrewd. He likes the odds. In a shootout, even if he's better he wants the odds. Won't take chances. Watch him."

Fargo gritted his teeth. "If I could only get close enough to do that."

Fargo waved at Dixon and went back to pick up the wagon trail. No point in streaking for Skytop Hill until the tracking proved it. The tracks did go south, and he pushed the pinto until it moved into its smooth strong stride that ate up the ground. And while he rode, he thought of Clay, a slimy hyena who wouldn't stand and fight, who used oversized bullies like Bigfoot, slimy toadies like Slick, and women as hostages.

He thought of the letter. If he didn't make trouble, nothing would happen to the women. Nothing, like what happened to Lily? You didn't trust a man like Clay. The last thing Fargo would do would be to ride off and leave Catherine, Teresa, and Elizabeth to the mercy of a mangy dog like Clay.

The trail veered off toward a giant hill; it would be Skytop Hill. They had driven the wagon like blazes for a time, then were forced here to rest the horses. From the prints of the boots, he read four men. Three on horseback, one on the wagon.

Clay was good at this sort of thing, he thought, grabbing women and making a run. He had never met Clay but felt he knew him through and through. How he looked, how he felt, how he thought. He was the kind of man who, wherever he went, leaked evil. Fargo craved nothing more than to get Clay in a face-to-face shootout.

The trail went up steeply, curved sharply, and the landscape was loaded with boulders, scrub bushes, trees, and tall grass. It was tricky terrain.

His trailing instinct flashed him a message of caution. He moved carefully behind a big boulder, dismounted, and scanned the hill. Three-quarters of a mile up, on top of the hill, perched a house. The boulders and tall grass offered plenty of cover for Clay's men as well as for him. If Clay was smart—and the bastard had proved it over and over—he'd spot his men behind the boulders, zigzag.

It meant a slow climb up. A rear piece of the wagon could be seen behind the house.

The women were probably in the house.

Were the men waiting with rifles behind those boulders?

Bet your ass, Fargo told himself. But he might have a few minutes' grace, this far down. He couldn't take the pinto up, and he'd be gone for a good time; there was grazing at a spot fifty feet to his left.

He moved the pinto out, heard the crack of a rifle, felt the burn on his left arm, and dropped. He dropped as if he'd been really hit, although it was a nick. He was behind a boulder, safe from another shot. He looked at the wound. The flesh was open and bleeding slowly. He peeled his kerchief, tied it tightly over the wound. Then he pulled his rifle from the saddle scabbard and sat silently.

He looked again at his arm. It leaked blood but was not serious. He had been foolish and made a mistake trying to move the horse; well, he made mistakes, like anyone else. The trouble was you weren't allowed mistakes, because mistakes kill.

He'd sit and wait. Clay would order a look. He wasn't the sort of man who could sit and rot, especially if he could risk other men.

Fargo decided then to let the pinto go out and graze; it would beef up their belief that he had caught the bullet.

He let go the reins, and the pinto, aware that he'd been given freedom to eat, drifted out toward the lush grass and began to nibble.

Fargo waited a few more minutes, then crawled on his stomach to the far end of the boulder. The grass there was tall, and he snaked into that, brought up his rifle, and waited.

Then he caught a glimpse of Slick, crouching low, running downhill for the nearest boulder. Fargo did nothing, watching the higher ground. There were Clay and three men. Perhaps another man, up higher, would also expose himself, then he'd know his position. But nobody showed. Only Slick, who obviously had been given orders to move up and check if he had scored a kill.

He raised his rifle and watched the boulder. It didn't take long. Slick felt safe, felt sure he had hit his man, and came out in a crouch for the next boulder. But he never made it; the bullet tore open the front of his chest and catapulted him back up the hill, where he fell, squirmed, and went still.

After firing, Fargo rolled back to the boulder and rushed to its other side to peer out. Halfway up the hill, the barrel of a rifle appeared, and two shots hit the grass spot where he'd been.

Fargo whistled for the pinto, which came in a quick canter to him behind the boulder. It was unwise to leave the horse out where they might shoot it to cut off his movement. They were the kind of scum to shoot a horse.

He didn't have much time. The trick was to keep pressure on the Clay bunch to keep them from turning on the women. Bullets have a way of grabbing the attention of men. He would crawl flat as a snake to the next boulder and. . . .

He sat still, leaning on the stone, aware that for the next few minutes nobody would make a move. Then he looked out. Someone behind a square rock thirty feet from the house started to crawl toward it. The target was too low, too fuzzy to see and kill, but he could be discouraged. Fargo put two bullets just in front of the movement. That stopped it. Nothing moved. To keep them pinned down, to stop reentry to the house, where the women had to be—that was the job.

He waited. It was always a waiting game. To move, yes, but at the right time. When it was least expected, like now. He began his slow crawl on the dirt path behind tall grass, taking great care not to make it stir.

He stopped crawling. He could smell the sun-scorched grass, could see black ants scurrying around a dead dragon fly. A yellowjacket hovered over him curiously, and he realized that even if it decided to sting, he couldn't swat it. Any move, now that he was in the open, would bring fire. The yellowjacket then decided there was nothing threatening in this human specimen and streaked off.

Now he could again concentrate. He knew the positions of two men, one with the rifle barrel, and the man in the flat black hat near the house. He must, as he crawled, keep these two positions fixed in his mind.

He crawled on his elbows, again only a few feet, aware that a change of his position gave him an edge. He closed his eyes to visualize the terrain. A thick-trunked oak sprouted from the ground about twenty feet to his left. If he reached it, it would give him an angle to pick off the man behind the boulder who had put out the rifle barrel.

He crawled a bit, waited, crawled again, waited. Then he heard a rifle shot that hit something thirty feet behind him. He grinned: nervous shooting at grass stirred by the wind. Three men up there were waiting for a hint of the target.

The light breeze which came in small spurts gave him a chance to elbow ahead at least five feet. Again he heard the crack of a rifle, but it was behind him. They were confused by the wind movement, and had strange ideas of his cover.

From his position, flat on the earth, behind the line of tall grass, he could see the oak, its branches soaring far out. He needed only a few more feet to reach the trunk. He set up his strategy of movement: shoot from the tree trunk, then run, using cover of the sagebrush, for the boulder about thirty feet up. That, of all moves, would be his riskiest. For at least five seconds he'd have no cover, and a sharpshooter, if ready, could pick him off. It was a calculated risk, but unavoidable. Otherwise he'd be stuck, pinned down in his position behind the tree trunk. And then all they had to do would be either to sweat him out or nail him from right and left, attacking at the same time.

He started for the trunk, and it was an agonizing crawl. He looked down at the black earth, and oddly, the thought of Lily came to him the day they had piled earth on top of her young broken body. He drew a deep breath. It was as if the spirit of Lily had come to him to fuel again his hatred of Clay and his quest to avenge her terrible death.

The wind lightly stirred the grass, and as he moved on his elbows the shadow of the tree trunk fell over him. Now he was there. He rose slowly to his knees then to his feet, aware of how sore were the muscles of his back from the crawling. He stretched his arms and body, then, with slow, very slow, movement brought his eye past the edge of the tree bark. There! That sidekick of Slick's, tough, muscular, his rifle held for sighting, peering at the boulder that Fargo had left long ago.

Up to his left, thirty feet off, was the boulder, his next port of call after he took care of this mangy dog; anyone who tied in with Clay could be nothing but that. From behind the trunk he brought up his rifle and moved out slowly to bring the target into his sights. As if the instinct of life always worked to discover danger, the man turned his head, looked directly at Fargo. And in the middle of the next second the center of his forehead split, and flesh, blood, and brain cascaded out, like a volcanic eruption. His knees turned to water as he went down.

Fargo, already in a crouch, was racing toward the great rounded stone, and each moment seemed a year. He expected gunfire, but instead he heard shouts, the sound of running, scuttling stones, then a shot that missed by an inch, splintered rock behind him. He flung himself down, breathing hard, for the run had been uphill. Listening, he heard more shouts, running. He could afford to catch his breath: he had a good position. There were only two left, Clay and his last man. And he would get them, oh yes, they wouldn't escape.

His arm felt wet and, looking at it, he was surprised to see that he was drenched with blood. The wound in his arm maybe was deeper than he had thought. He'd been unaware of it, but his blood loss was serious. More bandages and some rest were needed, not crawling up this damned hill on his elbows, which agitated the blood flow.

Well, he'd survive, he had a job to do and whatever else happened, Clay must go first.

It was then that he heard the horses, the crack of a whip, the yells of men, the screams of women, and the thundering sound of the wagon crunching over earth and stone.

He looked out.

It was the wagon pulled by horses that Clay had whipped into near panic, and they were rushing madly down directly at him. He glimpsed the women inside the wagon struggling to hang on to their seats.

He stared back at the house. Clay and a man in a black hat were on their horses, visible for just a moment as they rode down the other side of the hill. He brought up his rifle and fired without sighting, but it was a wasted shot. They were out of sight and gone. And what he had in front was a careening wagon pulled by half-crazed horses, and women locked inside screaming.

There was only one thing to do. He came out running, and as the lead bay horse swerved to avoid the boulder, slowing up, he caught the reins, pulled himself close, caught the mane of the horse, and swung over it. There was no stopping them, they would have to run out their fear. They took a path that traveled clear of the boulders, and he held the reins firmly and talked soothingly. Behind him the wagon jumped and rumbled, the women screeched, the horses neighed. This is right out of hell, he thought, as he tried to keep his voice gentle, talking to the horse, letting it run, stroking the neck, and thinking what a shrewd bastard Clay was, using the wagon for diversion for his getaway. Damn, it had worked, too. He wondered about the women. Had they been hurt? The way they screeched sounded healthy enough; it split his ears. Of course they thought the wagon would go over and they'd be dragged to their deaths. Well, he'd run the horses on the trail until they ran out.

He felt dizzy for a moment, and realized that pulling on the horses had caused a greater spurt of blood from his wound.

He gritted his teeth; now was the time to hang on

most, when it all looked rotten: weakness of the body, runaway horses, and the hard fact that Clay had gotten away.

He was thinking wildly, but still he had moved the horses onto the trail, and they were beginning to feel the push. The women had stopped their damned screeching, believing at last the wagon would not somersault.

He leaned forward, talked softly into the flattened ears of the bay. The ears came up, as if at last the horse was listening. Then he felt the slowdown; the horses had stopped snorting and were just running now. He pulled gently on the reins and got a response. Everything looked fine, and a moment later, the team was down to a walk.

He sat there, feeling the hot body of the bay, which heaved with each breath. He felt light-headed, stupid. He couldn't seem to move. He gaped at his arm. It looked like a great bloody stump, every inch of it red with blood.

Wonder if anything's left in my veins, he thought.

Then he saw Catherine in front of him, beautiful blond Catherine, staring at him.

"Oh, God, Fargo, you wonderful man. But what is it? You're shot! You're all bloody!"

The image of her shifted oddly in front of him. "Listen, my pinto is back there." His voice sounded far off. "We must get him." Then he fell off the horse and his brain went dark.

He sat up in bed, stared at the wall picture opposite him, the painting of sunset on the Alps, a mountain in Switzerland. He had been looking at that picture for three days lying in this bed, eating his meals, nagged to eat afternoon and evening by Catherine, who insisted on nursing him. Three damned days. On the first day, when he had found himself in the hotel room, the doctor had told Catherine that the bullet had cut an artery and he'd lost more blood than a slaughtered bull.

"He needs to lie around, to eat and build up blood again. Plenty of meat and rest."

He'd heard that and drunk some rotten-tasting medicine, and for the last three days had done nothing but eat, sleep, and dream.

His dreams were gory, all right, and always in the middle of them was one man, smirking.

He stretched, and it hit him that for the first time in three days, he felt right. Stronger, and clear in the head. He got out of bed. Yes, he felt clear in the head, and that was good.

He stood; he felt good. He got into his jeans and his buckskin shirt, pulled on his boots, then put on his hat.

The door opened. Catherine stared at him.

"Are you crazy?"

He strapped his gunbelt on.

"Yes, crazy to let Clay get three days on me."

She put her hands on her hips. "You have got to get well."

"I am well."

She looked at him. "An amazing man. Take two more days. Then you'll be right."

"It'll take three days' riding to catch up with him."

She shook her head. "Why don't you forget him, Fargo? You can't kill all the skunks in the world."

His eyes were stony. "He's the skunk I want to kill right now."

He leaned down to kiss her. "I'll be back to give you girls a proper goodbye."

"*If* you come back," she said, her blue eyes brimming with tears.

17

But it took two weeks before he could close in on Clay, tracking him from Skytop Hill south to Black Rock, where he lost the trail for almost a week. He picked up his trail again, finally, in Tombstone Corners, a lively colorful town he knew from a couple of stopovers.

It was not yet sundown, too early for the saloon, and he was passing the barbershop, where he saw Clancy sitting in his own barber chair, talking to a hanger-on. When Fargo walked in Clancy got out of the chair and picked up his scissors. He was potbellied, red-headed, wore an apron and a friendly grin.

"Hello, Fargo. Haven't seen you for a spell."

Fargo hung up his hat, sat down, and looked at his locks. "Don't do too much damage, Clancy."

Clancy waved his scissors proudly. "The best cutting man in the territory." He looked at Fargo's hair as a grizzly looked at horsemeat. He started to snip. "So, what's the news?"

"Same as always, Clancy. Just cut the hair right."

Clancy waved his hands, flourished them like an artist, and snipped away. "I hear rumblings about the Sioux. About war parties. Anything to it, Fargo?"

"I wouldn't take a wagon out," Fargo said.

"No, I reckon not. We need to get the cavalry out there," Clancy snipped away.

Fargo looked at him in the mirror. "Hey, Clancy, know a man called Clay?"

The barber stopped cutting, nodded, then went on cutting.

"Where do I find him?"

Clancy kept cutting while he talked. "Not a good man to find, Fargo. I saw him in a street fight just yesterday. In front of my window. Joe Riley, a smart kid, stopped him right out there. Told Clay he hated his guts, and to get out of town. Clay grinned and pulled his gun. It was greased lightning. Poor Riley never had a chance." He looked in the mirror. "I don't suppose Clay's a friend of yours?" He looked at Fargo's expression. "No, I didn't think so." He went on snipping. "Of course, you're Fargo." He grinned. "You never been beat in a draw either." He snipped, stepped back to admire his work. "So far," he added.

He started to comb Fargo's hair, patting it as he combed. "You can find Clay at Pete's Saloon. He's there every night with a deadhead called Smoky. Smoky, he's the burial party. They have fun, those two, killing the customers passing through. Clay's a credit to the name of our town. Tombstone Corners." He smiled broadly and pulled the apron off Fargo. "How do you like it?"

Fargo pulled out a silver dollar and dropped it in Clancy's hand. He looked at his reflection, then he said, "Anyone ever tell you, Clancy, that when you went into barbering, the butcher business lost a good man?" He reached for his hat, hanging on the peg.

"Tombstone Corners," he said, "It's a good place to plant a man like Clay."

As he went out, he noticed that Clancy was shaking his head. "Wish you luck—you're gonna need it," he muttered.

An hour after sundown, he started up the main street.

He stomped up the wooden stairs of the saloon, pushed open the swinging doors, and walked in. The smell of sawdust, whiskey, and cheap perfume hit him. There was a long bar with five drinkers, and a big card table under a green lamp, with players and four women, all rouged up. A black man at the piano was playing a dinky tune.

He walked to the bar.

Pete, the bartender, stout, with black hair plastered down and parted in the middle, came toward him, grinned to show a gap in his front teeth. He put out a shot glass, filled it.

"Well, Fargo, it's been a long time. Where you been?"

"On the trail, Pete." He slung down the whiskey. Pete refilled it.

"I'd hate to be out there right now, Fargo. I hear the Sioux are hittin' the wagons."

Fargo nodded, thought of Red Sun, and downed his drink.

Pete refilled the glass. "Run into any trouble?" he asked, his eyes shrewd.

Fargo thought of the dead settlers, the dead Sioux. He picked up the glass. "A little." The whiskey burned his throat, but it tasted good. He felt himself loosening.

"Little, huh? We know you, Fargo. Probably ran into a war party. That right?"

Fargo shrugged. "It's not a good time for the wagons."

Pete went down the bar to repeat Fargo's words and take care of other customers.

Fargo turned, put his elbows on the bar.

After a long dry run on the trail, he felt like pitching a fierce drunk. But first he had a score to settle.

The whiskey also seemed to oil his memories, and the image of Lily came back, chestnut hair, a sweet oval face, lovely as a fawn, with a quick smile for everyone, happy to be alive, to be moving into young womanhood, ready for love and for life.

All that snuffed out by a vicious killer.

His violent feeling about Clay, pushed to a corner of his mind while on the trail, boiled up again. Rage grabbed him like a physical thing, and he turned, poured another whiskey, gulped it, as if it would drown the fire of his anger.

There were vicious killers in the world, he thought, always had been, men who grabbed what they wanted and killed when they pleased. Men like that, with guns, ran amok among the good people, made them victims. Men like that fed their appetites, whatever the cost to others. And in a place like this, where the only law was the gun, men like Clay bullied the territory.

Well, there were men like him, too.

He caught Pete's eye.

"Does a man called Clay drop in here, Pete?"

"Clay?" Pete's blue eyes went stony. "Yeah. He comes

152

by. Every night about now." He mopped the bar. "Friend of yours, Fargo?"

It was curious, but it hit Fargo with a shock that he and Clay had never met each other, certainly not face to face, and didn't therefore know what each other looked like. Never a clear look.

"Friend, Pete? No, not exactly."

Pete smiled. "I thought not. Wish to hell he'd stop dropping in. Four kills last week. Settlers, riders. Drinks, gets ornery, picks a fight, and we're mopping up the floor. He's fast. The fastest gun around here. Oh, he spends a lot of money, always has it. But I wish he'd take his money somewhere else." He mopped the bar. "Speak of the devil," he muttered.

The doors had swung open and there, big as life, was Clay, and behind him a lean hatchet-faced man with a dead look.

Yes, Fargo had never seen Clay, but the description of him given by the men in the bank was burned into his mind. Big, powerful, a scowling face with quick dark eyes, a slit of a mouth, and the scars on his right cheek. He wore a flat black hat, black shirt, and two guns. Fargo was glad that he, too, had strapped on two guns.

Clay's dark eyes raked the saloon, and when they came to Fargo, stopped, stared at his face, his body, his guns. Clay's look was bold, hard, aggressive.

Fargo stared back, his lake-blue eyes cold as ice.

For a long moment they looked at each other, and it was clear Clay didn't like what he saw, but for the moment he decided not to challenge it. He walked to the bar, rapped with his knuckles.

"Wake up, wake up, Pete, you got a couple of thirsty men here." He turned to the hatchet-faced man, who had looked with hard eyes at Fargo. "Smoky," he said with a smile. It seemed to be a signal, for Smoky took a position at the bar about eight feet from Clay.

Pete, with a false smile, said, "Yes sir, Mr. Clay." And he poured three shot glasses in front of Clay. And one for Smoky.

Clay looked insolently at Fargo, then at the card table, then at the women. "Hello, Ruby," he said to a young, delicately built girl with rouged cheeks and blue eyes. She nodded at him. He smiled, and his smile was wolfish, then he downed the three drinks and tapped the bar. Pete refilled the glasses.

Clay drank two more, then took a deep breath and looked at the black piano player, who was smoking a cigar.

He turned to Smoky. "Hey, Smoky, we got a lazy nigger. Tell him to hit those keys. This place is like Charley's funeral parlor." He grinned at the men at the bar. They grinned back. They don't want to rile him, Fargo thought.

Smoky, a man who didn't smile ever, stared at the black man. "Aaron," he said.

Aaron began to play sweet music.

Clay turned to Smoky. "Tell him to put some kick in the music. We want lively music, not music to die by." He smiled wolfishly as he glanced around the bar. One of the men, a wrangler with a smooth pink face, wasn't smiling. Clay's eyes fastened on him.

"You didn't think that funny, Lacy, did you?"

Lacy was startled. "Oh, yes, Clay, I thought that funny."

Clay studied him. "But it wasn't funny. Dying ain't a funny business."

"Not for the sod who's dying," Lacy said with a smile.

"That's right, Lacy." His voice was cold. "I hear you don't like the way I treat Ruby. You think I'm rough on her. I heard you said that the other day. Didn't you?"

Lacy looked jolted. "Well, I may have said something. But I didn't mean anything."

Clay grinned, his cruel grin. "Oh, I know you didn't mean it. Otherwise, I'd feel mean. And I don't feel mean about you. But it was not a nice thing to say. You should remember that." He glanced at Smoky, who walked in front of Lacy, his hatchet face grim and unsmiling, and crashed a right to the jaw, which knocked Lacy against the bar, but he didn't go down. His lip sprang blood, and he held his mouth.

"You're lucky this time, Lacy," said Clay, his voice cold.

Lacy, his eyes shining with fear, held his jaw and walked through the swinging doors.

"Sorry for the unpleasantness, gents," Clay said, glancing at Fargo.

He picked up another shot, tossed it off, then looked at Ruby.

"Hey, Ruby, this is our music." He held out his hands, pulled her to the dance floor. "Music to make love by." He grinned at the men, then he stomped his boots, clapped his hands, and then slapped her butt, hard.

"Don't do that," she said sharply.

He stopped, his smile disappeared, and his eyes went cruel.

"What was that, Ruby?" He was all menace.

Sensing the danger, she blanched, then tried to smile. "I didn't mean anything, Clay. It hurt."

He stared, as if he'd rather feel mean, then decided her apology made it okay. "I thought you liked a little hurting, Ruby." He smiled, but his eyes looked cruel.

Her fear was obvious. "Please be nice, Clay. Please."

"Sure, sure, I'll be nice." He spread his hands, smiled at his audience, which watched him fascinated.

He's like a cobra, ready to strike anytime, thought Fargo.

"C'mere, Ruby, give Clay a little kiss."

She smiled, came close, and he grabbed her as if she were a sack of flour, put her over his knees, lifted her dress, pulled down her panties, exposing her buttocks, and started to spank her, his big hands making a resounding whack against her flesh.

She squirmed, she yelled, but he didn't stop until he had hit her eight times.

Nobody interfered.

Then he turned her and kissed her. "See, Ruby, you've been a naughty girl. You made Clay mad. You had to be punished. But I got no hard feelings, Ruby."

He turned to the men; they were all trying to smile. When he looked at Fargo, his eyes grew narrow.

"She's a great little piece. You should try her, mister."

"The name's Fargo." His tone was cold. He could feel nothing but ice and fury, watching Clay, but he was trying to make the right setup. Clay was in the center of the floor, in front of him, but to his sharp left stood the hatchet-faced man, Smoky, at the bar.

"Fargo!" His eyes widened almost with shock, and then, as if furious at himself for showing fear in front of others, and aware, too, that he had Smoky as a backup, his jaw hardened.

"I've heard of you, Fargo, yes. You been asking about me in places. Am I right?"

He turned to Smoky. "This is Fargo," and the signal was passed, as Fargo knew, as well as everyone in the room.

Smoky's face tried to grin; it was gruesome.

Clay looked stony. "You found me, Fargo. Now what do you want to say?"

The setup was all wrong, with Smoky sharp left like this. To draw now would be suicide; at least one of them would get a bullet in him.

A diversion. "I've just been watching you. You're kinda rough on women, Clay."

The tension went out of Clay's body. He, too, wasn't ready; in fact, he didn't mind talking to Fargo, a man who, for some time, had caused him trouble. Clay laughed. "Yeah, I'm rough on them. But they like it. And I like it."

He was cocky as a pixilated rooster. He had Smoky on the left and he was in front; they had the setup. Fargo had to move it around. Slowly Fargo picked up his drink, which turned him a bit toward Smoky.

Clay watched his every move like a hawk. He expects a shootout, but figures I don't like the odds, so he's talking, Fargo thought. He's in no hurry. Wants to know something of the man he's going to kill.

"You don't understand women, Fargo. They like to be kicked around, like dogs. Then they come crawling. And they act the way you like it. It's more fun that way."

This hyena was giving his sick view of love. How did someone like this get to crawl between heaven and earth?

The cardplayers had stopped playing, the drinkers had stopped drinking, the women had stopped talking. The tension in the saloon was thick.

"You've got a sick mind, Clay." Fargo put his glass on the bar.

Clay's face hardened, but he wasn't ready yet. He rubbed his chin, as if trying to think of something.

"Fargo, Fargo, what do we remember about Fargo, Smoky?"

After a long pause, "Some girl mentioned his name." Smoky's eyes were dark beads and riveted on Fargo. He knows we're on the edge and he's worried, Fargo thought as his body mobilized.

"Where was that?" asked Clay.

"Maybe I can tell you where, Clay."

"Yeah." Clay's eyes were glittery, and sweat glistened on his upper lip. "Do that."

Fargo spoke easily, though his eyes were icy. "It was back in Forked River. You're famous back there, Clay. You made a big withdrawal from the bank, you shot a couple of men. Then, you yellow-bellied bastard, you shot Lily Baines. A very good friend of mine."

When he finished, the room went dead silent, then everyone made a rush for the wall, pressed against it. And watched. A drama of death was about to happen.

Clay was staring, his mouth a vicious slit.

He couldn't believe Fargo would have the nerve. This man was calling him out, even though he knew the odds were against him. He stared into the icy blue eyes, felt a spasm of fear. Fear! But why? He had killed a lot of men, some with trickery, but he had never been beaten in a draw.

He had just been called a thief, a woman killer, and yellow.

Fargo had to be either crazy or the fastest gun in the territory. He had to be crazy.

His hand started down . . .

Those who watched never quite saw the movement of Fargo's hands, just the roar of his two guns.

Then they heard Clay's answering shot, but he was already dying, a great gaping hole pumping bright-red blood where his right eye had been. Smoky hadn't even cleared leather; he had been slung back by the big slug as if he'd been kicked by a mustang, the bullet hole in the center of his forehead, the back of his head gone.

Fargo looked down on Clay, not yet dead, on his knees, crawling toward Fargo, staring up with that great sightless eye. There was agony in his face, and amazement as the thought of his own death was happening in his brain.

Then he lay down flat, his face against the floor, still breathing, his hands twitching.

And he slowly, very slowly, died.

Later at the hotel back in Aberdeen, where he'd gone to say goodbye to the women, he saw them for the first time in regular city clothes. They wore long cotton dresses with flounces and swirls, but nothing could hide their womanly curves.

He had to smile when he realized that he had tasted each beautiful body, and each had been like a delicious piece of cake.

They all kissed him, and their eyes were misty.

Catherine walked with him alone to the pinto. She stroked the glossy neck of the horse, and as if it sensed this to be an emotional moment, the pinto nudged her and neighed softly.

Her blue eyes were deep with feeling.

"Why can't you stay, Fargo?"

His jaw tightened as he thought of why.

"I've got a job to do out there, Catherine. There's no way around it."

She leaned into him, her breast against him.

She kissed him, a long, sweet kiss, then touched his cheek and whispered, "Come back to Aberdeen soon. I'll be here waiting, Fargo."

He smiled down at her, climbed into the saddle, put the great horse into a canter, and headed out of town.

LOOKING FORWARD!

The following is the opening section
from the next novel in the exciting new
Trailsman series from Signet:

The Trailsman #17:
RIDE THE WILD SHADOW

*1861—the wild mountain basins
of the Absaroka Range where it crosses
the borders of the Montana and
Wyoming territories.*

She was sweet-faced, almost naked, the mayor's daughter, and in bed with him. She was also the damnedest surprise he'd had in years.

Skye Fargo pushed back black, unruly hair that fell over his forehead and knew that amazement still lined his chiseled, intense face as he watched the girl stretch languorously on the bed. Even clad so briefly as now, she retained that sweetly innocent air, as though she were a little girl playing grown-up. But her body was very grown-up, all beautifully curved, everything rounded, knees, hips, shoulders, graceful legs, modestly full breasts, everything pink-fleshed, nipples very pink, the circles behind each even pinker.

"What are you thinking, Fargo?" she asked, turning on her stomach, her smile mischievous.

"I'm thinking you've been a helluva surprise from the first day we met, Penny Wills," he said. She giggled and stretched again, and he let his mind go back to that first day. Hell, it wasn't even a week back. He'd brought a wagon of silver ore to town and been paid well for it. The town wasn't much of a place, an overgrown way station named Threadneedle because it sat between two mountains of the Absaroka Range on a narrow passageway. He'd gone to the general store to get himself a new pair of boots and she'd been there, buying a piece of yard goods, all dressed in pink cotton and a small pink parasol, looking like a stick of curvaceous cotton candy.

"I'm Penny Wills," she introduced herself with a bright smile. "Just get into town?" she asked, and he nodded.

"Strangers are easy to spot here," she said. "Especially handsome ones." He remembered taking her in, sensing something under that cotton-candy, sweet-faced exterior. Perhaps men, any men, were hard to come by in Threadneedle, he remembered thinking, and wondering, because it was a town that got a lot of men passing through.

"What do you do with handsome strangers?" he tossed out.

"That depends," she said with a quick smile. "Sometimes we go riding, picnicking, sometimes to a hoedown if there is one."

"Kind of hot for a hoedown," he remarked.

"Yes, it is hot. I could stand a drink," she said, and it was only the first of the surprises to come.

"I only saw one saloon. You wouldn't want to go there, would you?" he said.

"Why not? I'm the mayor's daughter. My father's Humphrey Wills. I can go anyplace I like in this town," she said.

They had the drink, then another, and he walked her to a modest house at the end of town. The rest followed not only quickly but with effortlessness on his part. They went riding the next day. She said she wanted to show him the beauty of the mountain range. She showed him a lot more. Once alone in the hills, she unbuttoned her shirt and rode with her breasts out, bouncing merrily in rhythm. "I like the feeling of freedom," she said. When they stopped to rest, she let him caress the pink-fleshed, lovely mounds, but she pulled away at anything more. He thought then that perhaps she was just a tease, one of those strange women who get their kicks out of tantalizing a man.

Nothing changed his mind the next day when they went into the lower hills of the Absaroka Range again, only this time her lips responded with more fervor and there were little moans as he pressed his mouth to the pink-fleshed mounds. But she pushed away again, sat back, her eyes studying him. "You're too handsome to let go by," she said. "But I like comfort, a big bed, a warm room, pillows and privacy. You don't know who might happen along out here."

"Such as Daddy?" he asked.

She gave her little-girl giggle. "There's a little hotel the other end of town. Get a room tomorrow night," she said. "I'll come by."

"I'll be there," he said. He followed her orders with eagerness pushing away surprise, feeling a little like a man who'd fallen into a gold mine. And now he watched her in the little hotel room as she rolled over to him, still keeping panties on. She let one hand move across the naked beauty of his hard-muscled physique, the powerful shoulders and broad chest, the long, rippling muscles of his thighs, and there was appreciation in her eyes.

"God, you're a piece of man," Penny Wills murmured.

He reached for her. "And you're a delicious little surprise package, Penny Wills," he said. He pulled her to him, and his hand caressed her breasts. He let his fingers move down across her curvaceous body, neared the dark triangle visible through the thin panties. His thumb hooked onto the edge of the garment, began to push it down, and her hand came at once to stop him.

"Not yet," she breathed. "I have to work up to it. I have to look, touch, feel, first."

He drew his hand away, brought it up to cup her breast, and with unexpected suddenness, she threw arms around him and lifted herself half over him, and he felt his swollenness hard against her belly. She rolled on her back, pulled him with her. "Ah . . ." she breathed. His hand went down to push away the thin panties, and then he heard the door burst open.

"Shit!" he swore, rolled from her, tried to reach the holster beside the bed with the big Colt .45 in it, but the voice froze him halfway across the bed.

"Don't try it, mister," the voice said. Slowly, Fargo turned to see the three figures that had burst into the room, each holding a rifle. He saw Penny pull her dress on with one quick motion as a fourth man strode into the room, pulling the door shut behind him. He fastened Fargo with an icy stare out of a hawklike face.

"You're in trouble," the man said. "You've taken my little girl."

"I didn't take anything, yet," Fargo said.

"In bed naked, laying on top of her, you were. How much more proof do I need?" the man said sternly. "An innocent young girl. You'll have to do right by her, now."

Fargo sat up, frowned at the man. "What the hell does that mean?" he shot back. He eyed the rifles again, decided there was no chance to make a move.

"It means you'll marry her, right here and now," the man said. "You violated her and you're going to make it right by her."

"What?" Fargo shouted. "You out of your damn mind?" He stood up, and one of the other men slammed the stock of his rifle into his stomach. He doubled over in pain, fell back onto the edge of the bed, hands to his midsection.

"Call Preacher Tooms," he heard the mayor say. One of the other men opened the door and shouted into the hallway. The preacher appeared at once, dressed in his black frock coat, Bible under one arm, a tall, dried-up-looking man. Fargo straightened up, fought down the pain in his stomach. "Put your pants on," one of the men ordered and watched with the rifle on him as Fargo pulled into his trousers.

"Wed this man to little Penny," the mayor said, and Fargo stood up and backed away from the man who'd slugged him. He saw Penny move to stand a little closer to him, and he stared at her with a frown of incredulousness.

"Now just a damn minute," he protested. "You can't do this. She came up here all on her own. Fact is, it was her idea."

"A young girl is easily lured into sin by a clever man,"

Humphrey Wills said. "We're ready, preacher," he said to the minister.

The man opened his Bible. "We are gathered here to join in holy matrimony these two young people," he began, and the mayor broke in brusquely.

"Cut all that and get on with it, Lemuel," he snapped.

The preacher turned a page in the book. "Do you, Penny Wills, take this man to be your lawfully wedded husband?" he read.

"I do," Fargo heard Penny say sweetly.

"Shit you do," he shouted. "You take that back, goddammit." He started toward her, and one of the men with a rifle stepped forward menacingly.

"Do you, Skye Fargo, take this woman to be your lawfully wedded wife?" the preacher went on.

"In a pig's ass," Fargo roared.

"He said 'I do,'" the mayor cut in. "I heard him. You hear him, boys?"

"We heard him," the three riflemen said.

"I pronounce you man and wife," the preacher said, snapping his Bible shut.

"Like hell you do. This is no wedding. This is a fucking farce," Fargo shouted. He watched Penny calmly start toward the door. "Goddam little bitch," he yelled. "You set me up."

Penny disappeared out the door, and her father's hawk face stepped in front of him. "You are legally married by the powers invested in Preacher Tooms," the man said calmly. "Finish dressing and the boys will bring you to my office." He turned and strode from the room. Fargo's eyes went to the three men. They held the rifles steady on him, and he watched one pick his gunbelt from the floor, sling it on his shoulder. He gathered up the rest of his clothes and dressed. One of the men gestured with the rifle to the hallway. Fargo walked from the room and felt the one man at his back, the other two falling in on each side.

They walked him from the hotel outside into the night street and a few hundred feet to a small, lighted office. He saw two barred cells behind the front room as he was taken inside. Mayor Humphrey Wills rose from behind a small wooden desk with his name in large letters, the word "mayor" even larger. "Sit down, Fargo," the mayor said as the three riflemen leaned against the wall. Fargo slid into the chair, glanced at the two cells and saw a man inside one, stretched out on the single cot. Fargo returned his eyes to the hawk-faced man in front of him.

"Now what the hell are you trying to pull off here?" he growled.

"Pull off? You have the wrong idea, Mr. Fargo. You violated my daughter and you had to do the right thing by her. You married her. You've been properly and legally married, by a preacher with witnesses," the man said.

"Proper and legal my ass," Fargo flared.

The man's face didn't change at his angry retort. He continued calmly, and Fargo began to realize it was a speech he had made many times before. "However, because of the powers of my office, and out of the compassion inside me, I can offer you a way out. I can annul this marriage. It will cost you five hundred dollars."

Fargo's lake-blue eyes stayed on the man, and he let his lips purse. A small, grim smile slid over his face. "Very nice," he murmured. "Really nice. How long did it take you to dream up this racket?"

Mayor Humphrey Wills stared back calmly. "Five hundred dollars," he said.

"I don't have five hundred dollars with me," Fargo said.

"You came in here leading an ore wagon. You were paid for that job," the man said.

"Three hundred dollars," Fargo said.

"You can give us that. Then you'll only have to spend six months on our work gang," the mayor said.

"Work gang?" Fargo frowned.

"You'll go wherever we send you, into the silver mines if they need extra help, logging camps, wherever," the man said.

"And if I don't pay up anything?" Fargo asked.

The man's hawk face wrinkled in thought for a moment. "I'd say you'd be on the work gang for three years," he replied casually.

"You sonofabitch," Fargo said.

"Five hundred dollars," the man repeated calmly. "Five hundred dollars and you're a free man." He leaned forward in the chair, his face growing harsher. "Let me spell it out more clearly for you. If you try running, every sheriff in every territory will get a notice that you're a runaway husband and wanted here. Every bounty hunter will get a notice of a price to bring you back. And it will be all perfectly legal and within our rights. You'll be a husband who has abandoned his wife, remember." He leaned back in in his chair. "By morning, you'll join all the others in my files at home, your marriage legally documented, signed by three witnesses, everything completely in order," he said.

"Bastard," Fargo said. Mayor Wills leaned forward in the chair and what passed for a smile crossed his face. "Now isn't it worth five hundred dollars to have all that off your back?" he said. Fargo stared at him in icy silence. "Three years on a work gang is a long time. Even six months," Major Wills said. "Most men quickly change their minds and find some way to get the money."

"And the others?" Fargo asked.

The man shrugged. "They're very helpful. Labor is in short supply around here," he said. Fargo felt the fury seething inside himself. "Give us the three hundred," the man said. "Six months isn't so long. Of course, you'll still be married then. You'll still have to come up with the money to have me annul that."

"Go to hell," Fargo said. "And take that pussy-waving little bitch daughter of yours with you."

The caricature of a smile came again. "Put Mr. Fargo in a cell, boys. We'll give him the night to think about his unwise reactions," he said, and Fargo felt the rifle prod him in the back at once. He was pushed into the cell with the man on the cot, the door was latched, and he turned to see the Mayor drop his Colt and the gunbelt into a drawer in the desk, slam it shut, and lock it. He watched the man turn the desk lamp down low before leaving the little office with the three riflemen. A lock was turned on the door from outside, and the mayor and his helpers disappeared from view.

Fargo turned, saw the man on the cot sitting up, a

young face, not more than nineteen, he guessed. "Welcome," the young man said, grim irony in the single word.

"You, too?" Fargo frowned.

The young man nodded. "Me and a lot of others," he said. Fargo's eyes moved around the cell, took in the corners, the edges where the bars fitted into the walls. "It's tight. There's no way out of here," the man said. "They don't make mistakes."

"They just did," Fargo said, and the man's eyes questioned. "They picked the wrong bridegroom," Fargo said through lips that hardly moved.

JOIN THE <u>TRAILSMAN</u> READER'S PANEL
AND PREVIEW NEW BOOKS

If you're a reader of <u>TRAILSMAN</u>, New American Library wants to bring you more of the type of books you enjoy. For this reason we're asking you to join <u>TRAILSMAN</u> Reader's Panel, to preview new books, so we can learn more about your reading tastes.

Please fill out and mail today. Your comments are appreciated.

1. The title of the last paperback book I bought was: _____

2. How many paperback books have you bought for yourself in the last six months?
☐ 1 to 3   ☐ 4 to 6   ☐ 10 to 20   ☐ 21 or more

3. What other paperback fiction have you read in the past six months? Please list titles: _____
_____
_____
_____

4. I usually buy my books at: (Check One or more)
☐ Book Store   ☐ Newsstand   ☐ Discount Store
☐ Supermarket   ☐ Drug Store   ☐ Department Store
☐ Other (Please specify)_____

5. I listen to radio regularly: (Check One)   ☐ Yes   ☐ No
My favorite station is:_____
I usually listen to radio (Circle One or more)   On way to work / During the day / Coming home from work / In the evening

6. I read magazines regularly: (Check One)   ☐ Yes   ☐ No
My favorite magazine is:_____

7. I read a newspaper regularly: (Check One)   ☐ Yes   ☐ No
My favorite newspaper is:_____
My favorite section of the newspaper is:_____

For our records, we need this information from all our Reader's Panel Members.
NAME:_____
ADDRESS:_____ ZIP_____
TELEPHONE: Area Code (   ) Number_____

8. (Check One)   ☐ Male   ☐ Female

9. Age (Check One)   ☐ 17 and under   ☐ 18 to 34
☐ 35 to 49   ☐ 50 to 64   ☐ 65 and over

10. Education (Check One)
☐ Now in high school   ☐ Graduated high school
☐ Now in college   ☐ Completed some college
☐ Graduated college

As our special thanks to all members of our Reader's Panel, we'll send a free gift of special interest to readers of <u>THE TRAILSMAN</u>.

Thank you. Please mail this in today.

NEW AMERICAN LIBRARY
PROMOTION DEPARTMENT
1633 BROADWAY
NEW YORK, NY 10019

SIGNET VISTA Books by Phyllis Whitney